THE FUTURE EVE

BY

VILLIERS DE L'ISLE ADAM

British Library Cataloguing-in-Publication Data
A catalogue record for this book is available from the
British Library

CONTENTS

CONTENTS

VILLIERS DE L'ISLE ADAM

Jean-Marie-Mathias-Philippe-Auguste, comte de Villiers de l'Isle-Adam, was born in Saint-Brieuc, Brittany, France in 1838. His family was a distinguished and aristocratic one, but they were not rich. During his youth, Villiers' father became obsessed with the notion that he could restore the family fortune by finding the lost treasure of the Knights of Malta, and spent large sums of money buying land, excavating it and then selling it at a loss when he failed to find anything of any value. As a result, the young Villiers' life and education was a fractured one, in which he attended almost ten separate schools. Despite this, he excelled in the arts, and his family became convinced he was an artistic genius.

During the late 1850s, Villiers spent a lot of time in Paris, where he became enthralled by artistic and theatrical life. Not long afterwards, he moved there permanently, eventually meeting his idol Baudelaire, who encouraged him to read the works of Edgar Allan Poe. In 1859, Villiers published his first work, a book of verse entitled *Premieres Poésies*. This went largely unnoticed, and it took Villiers another two decades to start publishing the works now regarded as his best – the short-story collection, *Contes cruels* (1883), the novel *L'Ève future* (1886), and the drama *Axël*

(1890). During these twenty years, Villiers was a commander in the Garde Nationale during the Franco-Prussian War, and spent much of his time in Paris avoiding creditors and taking bizarre and varied jobs to earn money.

Villiers works are fantastical in plot and filled with mystery and horror. They are now seen as both symbolist and romantic, in the style of Baudelaire and Poe. Villiers himself viewed *Axël* (published posthumously) as his masterpiece, although critics tend to consider *L'Ève future* his *magnum opus*. He died in 1889, having suffered from stomach cancer for a long time.

THE FUTURE EVE

Villiers De L'isle Adam

I.

TEN MILES FROM the great seething city there stands a large house in the centre of a network of electric wires, surrounded by wide, solitary grounds. A beautiful green park and shady, gravelled paths lead from the massive iron entrance gates to the isolated mansion. This was the home of the world-famed inventor and master electrician, Professor X.

The scientist, a man of about forty years, had more the appearance of a distinguished artist than a plodding scientist. It almost appeared that the face of the artist had been transformed into that of the inventor. The two had the same congenital aptitude with different applications, like mysterious twins who had developed their individual genius.

About five o'clock in the afternoon of a late autumn day the professor retired into the seclusion of his private laboratory, a small grey stone building standing in the rear of his large abode. A few minutes before he had dismissed his five pupils, devoted followers, scholarly and clever, upon whose discretion he could count, and who were his chief help in his scientific work.

Alone, seated in his great leather chair, a cigar in his mouth, his huge frame enveloped in a loose-fitting cloak of black silk, he seemed lost in thought. With eyes fixed and absent, he gazed into space, but his mind was working actively.

On his right was a high window opening toward the flaming west – the glowing sunset casting on all objects a red-gold mist. In the room were moulds of various shapes, instruments of precision, piles of blue prints, strange wheelwork, electrical apparatus, telescopes, reflectors, enormous magnets, bottles full of peculiar substances, slates covered with quotations.

Outside, from beyond the horizon, the setting sun threw its last rays on the curtain of maples and pines which overhung the steep cliffs near by, and illumined the room at moments with splashes of brilliance. The golden rays were reflected on all sides from crystal facets.

The air was keen. There had been a heavy storm during the day, and the rain had soaked the lawn and drenched the blown flowers in their green boxes under the windows. Creeping plants and ferns hung somewhat awry from their iron baskets, due to the violence of the storm. In the subtle urge of this atmosphere, the strong and keenly vivacious thoughts of the scientist became attenuated, influenced by the meditative spirit – and the twilight.

Although the inventor's hair was greying on the temples, his face was boyish, his smile was frank and winning. Around his mouth were little lines which told of the struggles and hardships which he had encountered in the early days of his career. It had been bitter uphill work, but he now stood on the pinnacle of fame; he was positive in his opinions, espousing even the most specious of theories only when duly bulwarked in facts. A humanitarian, he was prouder of his labours than of his genius.

Like an ordinary mortal, he sometimes abandoned himself to most fantastic and bizarre reflections. And now he communed with his ego, humbly, sadly.

'How late I come in humanity's history,' he mused. 'I should have been born centuries ago. Alas, I have come into this world very late.'

He arose from his chair and began to pace up and down the laboratory as he thought of the great happenings of olden days which could have been turned to the world's advantage. In the midst of his meditations he heard the voice of a young woman speaking softly near him.

'Master!' came the murmur.

And as yet there was not the shadow of a form to be seen.

The professor had started at the ghostly sound.

'You, Sowana?' he asked aloud.

'Yes,' said the voice. 'This evening I needed a good sound sleep, so I took the ring. I have it on my finger now. There is no occasion for you to raise your voice to its natural pitch. I am quite near you, and, for the last few minutes, I have been listening to you speaking your thoughts aloud like a child.'

'Yes, Sowana. But, bodily, where are you?'

'I am stretched out on the fur rugs in the vault behind the bush where the birds are.

'Hadaly seems to be asleep. I have given her some lozenges and some pure water, and – well, they have made her quite *animated*.'

The invisible being whom the inventor had called Sowana laughed as she uttered the last word. Her voice, discreet and low, came from the folds of a velvet curtain, carried from the distance by the electrical current in the sonorous, vibrating plaque in the portières; one of the professor's new condensators through which the pronunciation and the tone of the voice were distinctly transmitted.

'Tell me, Mrs Anderson,' he resumed, 'are you sure that you can hear what another person says to me in this room – now, in the state that you are in?'

'Yes, if you speak distinctly, very low, between your lips, the difference in the intonation between your voice and the replies enables me to understand the dialogue absolutely. You see, I am like one of the jinn of the ring in the "Thousand and One Nights." '

'Then, if that is the case, if I were to ask you to attach the telephone wire by which you speak to me, at this moment, to the person of our beautiful young friend, the miracle in which we are both interested would take place?'

'Without the slightest doubt. I am positive of it,' declared the voice. 'It is a prodigious thing, ingenious and ideal, but, worked out according to these calculations, it will come about naturally.

'Now,' continued the voice, 'for me to be able to hear you in this marvellous state in which I am at this moment; penetrated as I am with the living fluid in the ring, there is no need for you to have a telephone; but in order that you or any of your visitors should hear me, the mouthpiece of the telephone which I am holding now must be in connection with something which will correspond with the metal sounding plate, no matter how hidden it may be. Is that right?'

'That is exactly right. And now, Mrs Anderson, tell me –'

'Oh!' cried the invisible speaker, with a plaintive catch in her voice. 'Gall me by my dream name *here*. I am another being now, not myself. Here I forget my sorrows, and I do not suffer. The other name recalls the horrible things of earth to which I still belong.'

'I will do as you wish, Sowana,' said the professor gravely. 'Now I want you to tell me – you are quite sure of Hadaly, are you not?'

'Ah,' replied Sowana, 'you have given me so much information about your beautiful Hadaly, and I have studied her so thoroughly, that I can reply – well, as I would for my own reflection in a mirror! I would rather exist in that vibrating creature than in my own self.

'What a sublime creation you have, my dear master! She exists in the superior state in which I am at this moment. She is imbued with our two wills; they are united in her; it is a dualism – not conscious – a spirit. When she says to me, "I am a phantom," I feel embarrassed. You know, professor, I have a presentiment – I believe that Hadaly will be incarnated, actually turning to flesh and blood!'

'Ah' said the great electrician, with a little gasp, 'if such a thing could come to pass – but alas, I do not see how that could be!

'Go and sleep now, Sowana,' he continued in a low voice which was almost a whisper; 'but you know that there must be a third living being, in order that Hadaly should become incarnated. The masterpiece could not be produced without a third, and who is there on this earth that we would dare to consider worthy?'

'Yes, that is true,' murmured Sowana, 'but we shall see. I

believe that it will take place.'

There was a slight pause, and then the voice, in the tone of one who is dropping off to sleep, murmured:

'This evening I shall be ready, master. A flash, and Hadaly will appear. All will be well.'

Then came a mysterious silence after this conversation which was as strange as it was incomprehensible. The engineer stood in the middle of his laboratory with his arms folded across his chest. There was not a sound to be heard now, only, every now and then, a slight inward catch of his breath, as he dwelt on the meaning of the last words Sowana had spoken.

'She thinks Hadaly will be incarnated,' he mused. 'Although I have long familiarized myself with this phenomenon, there are times when I become dizzy, and my brain whirls when I think about it. Sowana believes that Hadaly will be incarnated. How could that be? The speech – aye, that's it – the speech – although I have reproduced the voice in a phonograph, how can I make that voice human? Ah, but science –'

The professor's eyes glowed like fire as he mused thus. He laughed aloud. Why did this great inventor now appear to treat the tremendous problem so lightly, so gaily? He was probing the depths of a great puzzle, but it did not appear now to baffle him completely, for he continued to smile.

Geniuses are so made. It seems almost as if they endeavour to make their brain whirl with their own prodigious thoughts.

They wander through the labyrinths of science, and then in a moment, in a flash, they perceive that for which they are seeking. No wonder they appear absentminded, for their thoughts are far away from matters of the everyday world.

The shadows around him deepened, for night had fallen.

Still meditating, the wizard inventor switched on a soft, pale light which dimly illumined the great laboratory. Then he lit a second cigar.

He was still in the midst of his reveries when the silence was broken by a clear ring. Going to a phonograph, the resonating plate of which was connected to a telephone, he set in action the metal disk, which relieved him of the necessity of replying in person, for the great man avoided speaking as much as possible to others.

'Well, what is it?' cried the instrument into the mouthpiece of the telephone with the voice of the inventor, slightly impatient. 'Is that you, Martin?'

'Yes, sir. I am in the city, at your office. I am sending you a telegram which came this moment.'

The voice came from the apparatus of a perfect condensator, the secret of which Professor X had not yet divulged to the world, a polyhedral ball suspended from an induction cord which hung from the ceiling.

The professor glanced toward the receiver of a Morse instrument which was standing on a base close to the telephone.

It held a telegraph blank.

There was an almost imperceptible fluttering which slightly agitated the double corresponding wires, and the professor stretched out his hand for the paper, which was shot out of its metal socket. Holding the telegram to the light, he read:

Arrived this morning. Hope to see you this evening. Affectionate greetings.

EWALD

Professor X gave a start of pleased surprise when he read the signature.

'Lord Ewald!' he cried. 'So he has come back to this country. Well, I am delighted.'

He continued to smile, and, in his smile, one could not have recognized the sceptic of the few previous moments.

'Ah, my dear, young friend,' he murmured, 'I have not forgotten you. At the time when I most needed a friend, you came – you gave aid to a stranger. It is hardly likely that I could forget my benefactor.'

The professor walked hastily over to a drapery and touched an electric button. The sound of a bell rang out in the park near the great house. Then, almost at once, the gay, happy voice of a little girl was heard.

'What do you want, papa?' she asked.

He seized the mouthpiece of an instrument that was placed between the draperies.

'Lord Ewald will call here this evening,' he said; 'tell the servants that I am expecting him, and that he can enter. He must be made to feel quite at home.'

'Very well, father,' replied the same happy voice, which, owing to a placing of the condensators, appeared to come, this time, from a big reflector of magnesium.

'I will let you know if he will have supper with me,' continued the inventor. 'Do not wait up for me, and mind you be a good little girl. Good night, darling.'

A charming, childish trill of laughter seemed to come from the shadows on all sides; it was as if an invisible elf in the air had replied to the inventor. He smilingly dropped the receiver, and resumed his striding up and down the room.

As he passed near an ebony table upon which various instruments were strewn, he carelessly threw down the telegram he had just received. By chance, the slip of paper happened to fall upon an extraordinary object, a startling object, the presence of which was unexplainable in this room.

The circumstance of this casual encounter of the telegram and this object attracted the scientist's attention. He suddenly stopped his striding, considered the fact, gazed intently at the object and the telegram, and, then, became thoughtful indeed.

II.

It was a human arm and hand lying on a violet silk cushion. The blood appeared to be congealed around the humeral section. Some crimson splashes on a piece of white linen, which had been thrown down beside it, attested to a recent operation.

It was the arm and hand of a young woman.

A bracelet of chased gold, in the form of a serpent, was clasped around the delicate wrist. On the ring finger of this left hand a sapphire ring flashed brilliantly. And the exquisitely slim fingers still retained their hold on a pearl-grey glove which, evidently, had been worn several times.

The flesh was so lifelike in tint, so soft and satiny, that the sight of it was poignantly cruel.

What could have necessitated this drastic, desperate operation? What unknown, terrible harm could have brought about this frightful amputation? And, above all, what had caused this arm to retain its healthy vitality? The blood still seemed to flow in this sweet and gracious member.

But a chilling, sinister thought would have leaped in the mind of a stranger at the sight of it.

The large country house which stood alone like a gloomy

castle among the trees was an isolated abode, and Professor X, as all the world knows, a daring experimenter. It was only to his closest friends that he showed any signs of affection.

His discoveries as an engineer; his inventions of various kinds, the least strange of which are alone known to the general public; conveyed the impression of an enigmatic positivism.

He had compounded an anaesthetic so powerful in its effect that, in speaking of it, his flatterers said: 'If only one had the time to absorb a few drops of it, one could face the most subtle tortures without being aware of it.' And, now, was he trying a new experiment, before which a doctor might well flinch? Was he striving to fathom the existence of another? Or was he trying to solve his own?

What scientist, worthy of the title, would not, if only for a moment, dwell without remorse, and even without shame, on thoughts of this order, when it was a question of a great discovery?

The press, all over the world, had given much space to describing the nature of some of his experiments. Many of the tests which he had desired to make had been forbidden by the government of his country.

A layman might feel, legitimately, a suspicion that the great scientist had been trying some experiment which had ended fatally, some venture of which this beautiful, radiant arm, rudely severed from its place, was the souvenir.

Meanwhile, as he stood beside the ebony table, Professor X looked meditatively at the telegram which had fallen between two fingers on the hand. He touched the hand, and, then, he started, as though a sudden idea had come to him.

'Ah,' he murmured, 'suppose it should happen, suppose – suppose that Lord Ewald – suppose it is he who will be the one to awaken Hadaly.'

The word 'awaken' was uttered by the scientist in a rather odd, hesitating manner. After a moment he shrugged his shoulders and smiled.

'Bah!' he muttered. 'I must not let my thoughts race ahead in this fashion.'

He resumed his striding up and down the laboratory. He evidently preferred to be in the dark, for he switched off the lights.

Suddenly the moon passed between the clouds, and sinisterly slipped a streak of light onto the black table.

The pale ray caressed the inanimate hand, lingered on the arm, and threw a gleam into the eyes of the gold snake and a flash on the ring.

Then all became dark again.

Professor X pondered, as he paced to and fro in the darkness, upon all the wonderful inventions he had given to the world.

He thought of all the great scientists of the past; those famous engineers who built the temple of Cheops, and all the other wonders which have been left to endure through the ages; of the architects who had left their imprint on colossal, marvellous ruins which were, even now, masterpieces unexcelled. Was it not strange that some of these deep minds had not conceived the things which he had perfected?

As his mind passed down through the cycles of history, he conjured up pictures of the marvellous men and women whose names have been inspiring to us. How beneficial it would be if we could have had preserved for us their actual photographs. What a loss that this art had been so long deferred!

What remarkable progress might have been made possible if we only had actual photographic records of the progressions of natural history. How quickly nature had effaced the traces of her first efforts. What precious visions had been lost!

And he felt a great feeling of thankfulness within him. A thankfulness that, because of his having existed, because of his inventions, mankind would henceforth reap great benefits.

And, more than that, if it were possible – if the great God, the Lord of Life, of whom so many painters and sculptors had tried to give us an image – if this Mighty, Most High would but permit a photograph of Himself to be taken, would but permit the sound of His voice to be recorded, from that day on there would not be left an atheist on the face of the earth.

As it was his habit, the professor had been softly speaking his thoughts aloud as he paced to and fro in the laboratory. He now stopped and looked absently through the openings of the long French windows, staring at the rays of light which the moon cast across the lawn.

'So be it,' he murmured, resuming his soliloquy. 'Let it be defiance for defiance. Since life will not deign to answer our questions, but treats all our inquiries with a profound and problematic silence, we will defy life-creation. I have already taken the prodigious step, and now have something to show.'

At this moment, the professor caught sight of a human shadow through the glass doors.

'Who is there?' he cried, his fingers closing over the butt of a small revolver in his pocket.

'It is I – Ewald,' replied a voice.

'My dear Lord Ewald. Welcome!' cried the professor, as he came forward to greet his guest.

Three unusually large lamps, with globes of blue glass, simultaneously burst into flame like huge torches of electricity, lighting up the laboratory.

The visitor was about twenty-seven years old, tall, manly, and extremely handsome. He was immaculately groomed, and his magnificent physique suggested his apprenticeship on the crews of Oxford or Cambridge.

His face, calm in repose, was sympathetic in expression,

but the look in his eyes was grave and somewhat haughty.

'My dear friend,' said the inventor. 'All that I now have I owe to you, for, without the help you once gave me, I could have accomplished nothing.'

'No, no, professor,' said Lord Ewald, smiling, 'it is I who am indebted to you. Through you I was able to be useful to the rest of humanity. The bit of money meant nothing to me.

'See how fortunate I consider myself in having met you! As soon as I put foot in your country I hasten to call to see you, for I want to renew the friendship that began with a chance meeting.'

Professor X now suddenly detected that there was something subtly wrong with his guest.

'I see you think that I am ill,' continued the younger man, with a slight understanding smile. 'I am not suffering physically, I assure you. But I have an everlasting grief and, I suppose, that would make one look a bit off in the course of time.'

Lord Ewald glanced about the perfectly appointed laboratory, paying particular attention to the lighting.

'I must congratulate you on all that you have accomplished in such a short time,' he continued. 'You are certainly the chosen one – a veritable genius. This marvellous lighting is your own invention, I presume?'

The professor nodded.

'It is like a brilliant afternoon in summer time,' said his lordship.

'Again thanks to you,' his host declared with a smile.

'It is all very wonderful; you are an electrical wizard.'

'Well,' said the professor modestly, 'I have discovered a few little things – and also some important things that I want to tell you about. I was just thinking, before you arrived, that my inventions should have been known centuries ago.'

Lord Ewald listened politely to his host, but it was evident that his secret sorrow obsessed him. The professor's keen eyes scanned the young man's face searchingly. There was a moment's silence.

'My dear Lord Ewald,' said the inventor, gravely, 'permit me to assume the rôle of an old friend and interest myself in you. I can see there is something very wrong. Your trouble?'

The younger man tapped the cold ashes from his cigar, and looked at his host, but said nothing.

'You know that I am a physician also,' continued the professor, 'and I am one of those who believe that there is a remedy for every illness.'

'Oh, the grief in question,' responded Lord Ewald, trying to speak lightly, 'is a very commonplace subject – an unfortunate love affair. It has hit me hard. You see, now, that my secret is very ordinary. I shall always suffer, but, please, do not let us speak about it.'

'*You* unfortunate in a love affair!' cried the doctor, in astonishment. 'You the victim! Why, that almost seems impossible. I –'

'Pardon me,' interrupted his young friend, 'I have only a short time to spend with you and I do not wish to abuse your time. I think the conversation will be far more interesting if we talk of you and what you have accomplished.'

'Why, my time is all yours!' cried the inventor. 'Those who admire and laud me to-day once ignored me and would have allowed me to die like a homeless dog – all but you.

'My affection for you is sincere, and it has rights which are just as sacred as yours, my dear young friend. Perhaps I may be able to cure you, or, at least –'

'No,' interrupted Lord Ewald, with a bitter smile, 'unfortunately, you can do nothing – science cannot go as far as that.'

'One never knows,' declared the professor. 'Science has astonished me. I am always working – always probing – always discovering. Who can tell?'

'I know that you could not understand the sentiment I have in this affair,' the young man demurred. 'It would be strange – inconceivable to you.'

'So much the better,' exclaimed the professor. 'It will be a challenge to my imagination.'

III.

Lord Ewald settled back in his chair, crossed his legs, and after relighting his cigar, spoke as follows:

'For some years past I have been living at Athelwold Castle, one of the oldest estates in England. It is surrounded by pines, lakes, and rocky hills.

'Since my return from an expedition into Abyssinia, I have led an isolated existence there. My parents are dead, and the only other persons in the castle with me are a few servants who have grown old in our service.

'One morning I had occasion to run up to London. There were few vacant compartments in the train. At one of the stations, a young lady, after looking hastily everywhere else for a seat, jumped into the carriage where I was seated.

'I need not go into details. In a brief time we became the best of friends. I fell in love with her.

'Alicia Cleary was only twenty years of age. She was a Venus, exquisite in form and face. It was the beauty of the Venus of Milo come to life – or the Venus Victrix.

'Her heavy brown hair, which hung about her like a mantle, had the radiance of a summer night. Her face was an exquisite oval. Her hands were not quite as aristocratic as the rest of her form, but her feet had the same eloquence as the Greek statues.

'Her eyes were beautiful, her brows perfectly shaped. The sound of her low voice was so thrilling, the notes of her songs so stirring, that I was overcome with a strange emotion. My admiration, as you shall see, was of an unknown order.

'In London, at the different Court functions, I had met the most beautiful girls in England, but I scarcely noticed them. I had thoughts of Alicia only.

'From the first days, however, I struggled to combat the peculiar evidences which appeared in her words and actions. I told myself that it was folly to admit their significance, and I sought in every way to put them from my thoughts.

'Yet, I could not forget that in all living beings there is a depth, which gives to their ideas, even the most vague, and to all their impressions, those modifications which are shown externally. This depth gives them their aspect, colour and character; it is in fact the inflection of their true selves. Let us call this substrata the soul, if you wish.

'And, between the body and soul of Alicia Cleary, there was a disproportion which disconcerted me.'

When Lord Ewald made this statement, the professor barely hid a start of surprise. His face paled, but he did not voice his agitation.

'It seemed,' continued Lord Ewald, 'that her inner self was

in absolute contradiction to her beautiful form. Her beauty was quite foreign to her words, her conversation appeared out of place in such a voice.

'It seemed that her peculiar personality was not only deprived of what is called by philosophers the "plastic mediator," but actually imprisoned, by a sort of occult punishment, in her body. It is a perpetual contradiction of her ideal beauty.

'Yes, sometimes, I seriously think that this woman has strayed by mistake into the form of the goddess – that this body does not belong to her!'

'An extreme supposition,' murmured the scientist, 'but it is a thought not at all rare. Similar feelings are often evoked in the hearts of those who are in love for the first time. It is, however, probable that Alicia's sublime beauty was not in keeping with the smallness of her soul. You will pardon me, but has this beautiful creature been faithful to you?'

'I would to heaven that she had!' exclaimed Lord Ewald, bitterly. 'No; but I believe that I have the only love of which she is capable.'

'Ah,' said the scientist soberly, 'please go on.'

'I learned that she came from a good family and that her betrothed had forsaken her to marry a girl with a fortune. Alicia left home, intending to lead a Bohemian life as a singer. However, she later gave up this idea.

'Her voice, appearance, and dramatic talent would have

provided her with an income sufficient for her needs. But she was glad to have met me just when she was setting forth into the world. She could not be my wife, she said, but she was eager to accept the love and protection which I pressed upon her.'

'Well, at least, that was an honest confession,' said the professor.

Lord Ewald appeared to be approaching a painful part of his story. However, he continued calmly:

'Yes, but that is my version that you have just heard, not hers. She spoke in other words, in another style. I suppose I shall have to speak more clearly so that you may understand her character better.

'What she really told me was that her betrothed was a fickle lover. His status was that of a small manufacturer, and she had been hopeful of marrying him solely because he had a certain amount of money.

'She certainly did not love him, yet she pretended that hers was a *grande passion*. Her plans to ensnare him with her blandishments went astray, however, so she fled from the gossip of the town and hurried to London intending to go on the stage, but, having met me, she changed her mind.

'She told me quite frankly that she was well pleased to have met me. I could see that the fact that I had a title delighted her immensely. Now, after this version, what do you think of her?'

'Well,' said the professor, with a cynical smile, 'your version and hers are different, in truth.'

There was a moment of silence.

'My thoughts are dwelling on the fundamental senses,' resumed Lord Ewald. 'How can this young creature, so wonderfully beautiful, be utterly unappreciative of herself. How can she ignore the divinity – the exquisite perfection – which her body represents?

'How can she fail to have lofty aspirations – high ideals? To her these wondrous things do not exist; she only forces herself, in a sort of shamefaced manner, to assume them.

'Her golden voice is only an empty instrument to her; she considers it merely as a means of livelihood to make use of when all other means have failed. The happiness that she could give to others with it means nothing to her.

'She so lacks a sense of shame that she delights in relating her unfortunate love affair to me. If she had a remnant of tact it should warn her that she is destroying all the sympathy and admiration that I could have for her.

'This beauty that should be inspiring is so steeped in moral blindness that I am forced to renounce it. I cannot love a woman who has no soul.'

Lord Ewald paused abruptly.

The professor, however, blithely nodded his head as a sign

for him to continue. The analysis of Miss Cleary's character apparently gave the listener much pleasure.

'When Alicia is not speaking,' the young nobleman went on, 'and her face is not wearing the expression which her empty, unprincipled remarks call forth, she is divine. Her wondrous beauty then gives the lie to all the base things that she has voiced.

'With a person who is very beautiful, but of ordinary perfection, I should not have this unexplainable sensation which Miss Cleary causes me? I would have known from the beginning – the quality of the lines, the texture of the skin, the coarseness of the hair, a movement, any of these tiny signs would have warned me of the hidden nature – and I should have recognized her identity with *herself*.

'But Alicia's beauty is the Irreproachable, defying the most minute analysis. Exteriorly, from head to feet, she is a veritable Venus Anadyomene; inside, the personality, the *soul*, is entirely foreign to the form.

'Imagine a *commonplace* goddess! I have come to the conclusion that all physiological laws were overthrown in this living, hybrid phenomenon.'

'My dear friend, you are certainly a poet,' declared the professor. 'Disillusionment must have been indeed severe, since it forced you into the heights of poesy to describe the commonplace truth. Your words are as fantastic as the story of a grand opera.'

'Yes, my subtle confessor,' the young man agreed bitterly, 'I know – I am a dreamer, but I have been well punished for my dreams.'

'But,' asked the professor, 'how is it that you are still in love with her, if you are able to analyse her character so correctly?'

'The awakening from a dream does not always bring forgetfulness,' replied Lord Ewald, sadly. 'Man is enchained with his own imagination. That is how it is in my case. I cannot break the tie now that I have awakened. My Delilah has cut my hair during my sleep.

'She does not know what attacks of rage and despair I have to control on her account. There are moments when I feel that I would like to kill her and then destroy myself.

'A mirage has enslaved me to this marvellous, living form with a dead soul. Alicia, to-day, represents for me simply the habit of a presence. I swear that it would be impossible for me to desire her.'

The professor started as if to speak, but hesitated as the disconsolate lover added:

'Yes, we exist together, but we are separated forever.'

Silence fell between the two men.

'Now, just a few questions,' said the professor finally. 'Is Miss Cleary a stupid person?'

'Certainly not,' declared Lord Ewald, smiling slightly.

'There is no trace of that stupidity which is almost saintly. She is not stupid, she is just silly.'

'I understand,' said the scientist. 'A little foolish, insipid. But she has talent, has she not?'

'Great heavens! I should say so!' exclaimed Lord Ewald. 'She is a virtuoso – the direct and mortal enemy of genius and art, in consequence. Art has no bearing, you know, with the virtuoso, neither is genius related to talent.

'Her voice is wonderful, but she will never sing unless I beg her to do so. It bores her to sing, for she considers it only as a part of a profession – one might say, as *work*, for which she does not consider that she was made.'

'Well, the fact is,' said the professor, 'one can't make a horse run fast merely by the fact that it has been entered in a race. Only, it is positively remarkable to me that, in spite of the depth of this analysis of character, you do not perceive that this lady would be the feminine ideal for three-fourths of humanity.'

'But it is killing me,' said Lord Ewald.

Then, giving way to a boyish impulse, which until then he had controlled, he cried:

'Oh, who could put a Soul into that body!'

IV.

At Lord Ewald's impulsive words a strange gleam, the light of genius, leaped into the professor's grey eyes. He drew in his breath with a slight hissing sound which betrayed the deep emotion he was feeling. But the younger man was too absorbed in his thoughts to heed these signs.

'Yes,' continued Lord Ewald, almost reminiscently, 'I thought I could change her. I tried to give her healthy diversion; I treated her as a sick person.

'I hoped that travelling would educate and improve her mind. But, in Italy, in France, in Spain, it was just the same. She looked jealously at the masterpieces, which she thought deprived her, for the moment, of complete attention, without understanding that she, herself, was a part of the beauty of those masterpieces, without knowing that they were but mirrors, reflecting her own reflection, that I was showing her.

'In Switzerland, we watched the sun rising over the mountains, but, instead of being inspired by the sight, she cried out, with a smile that was as radiant as the sunshine itself: "Oh, I hate these mountains; they just seem to want to crush me."

'In Florence, while we were standing before the wonders of the century of Leon X, she yawned slowly, and said: "Quite interesting, isn't it?"

'Once we were at a concert, listening to Wagner. She wanted to leave before it was half over, exclaiming petulantly: "Oh, I can't get the tune of this music. It is just a lot of bangs, just noise – it's just crazy!" If her sublime face could have portrayed the expression of her soul, she would have worn a distorted grimace.

'In Paris, I had the keenest desire to show this living woman the great statue of Venus – her very image. I wanted to see what she would say in the presence of her counterpart. I said to her, half jokingly: "Alicia, I am going to take you to the Louvre galleries, and I think that you will see something there that will surprise you."

'We walked through the halls, and, then, quite suddenly, I led her into the presence of the eternal statue.

'This time she raised her veil and gazed at the marble figure with a degree of astonishment, as she cried out naively: "Why, that's me!"

'I said nothing. I waited. After a few moments' stupefied pause, she looked at me and said: "Yes, that's me, except that I have not lost my arms, and I am much more aristocratic-looking." Then she shivered a little; she had withdrawn her hand from my arm and was holding the balustrade.

'She now took my arm again, and said, in a low tone: "Oh, these statues, these stones here make me feel so cold. Come on, let's leave!"

'Once outside the historical building, I glanced at her, for she had been silent for some minutes and I had a sort of hope that she had been stirred. She had been stirred, indeed, but – how? After thinking for some time, she came quite close to me and said: "If they make so much fuss over that statue, I ought to be a tremendous success."

'I confess that her words gave me a queer feeling. Her foolishness soared as high as the heavens; it seemed like a damnation. I simply said: "I hope so!"

'I escorted her to her hotel. This duty accomplished, I returned to the museum and again entered the sacred halls. I looked at the goddess, and, then, for the first time in my life, I felt my heart ready to burst with one of those mysterious dry sobs that stifle a human being.

'Picture, then, this woman, an animated duality which repelled and attracted me. My ardent love for her beautiful voice and her exterior charms is now entirely platonic.

'Her moral being has frozen the fires of my senses forever; they have become purely contemplative. I am only attached to her by a sorrowful admiration. I would like to see her dead, if Death would not efface those human features.

'There is nothing that can make Alicia Cleary worthy of a great love. My only wish for her now is to have her go on the stage to the career she desires, and then there will be nothing more in life for me.

'There you have the story. You can see there is no remedy. I must be going. This is good-by. I shall never return.'

'Wait a moment, my dear young friend,' said the professor sharply. 'I can see that you are contemplating a serious step on account of a woman. Bah! It is nonsense.'

'I loved Alicia,' Lord Ewald declared quietly as he arose; 'she represented to me everything that was divine and beautiful.'

The professor saw that the manly youth standing before him had the thought of suicide well defined in his mind.

'Lord Ewald,' he said, sternly, 'you are only the victim of a youthful passion which you have idealized. Time will cure you. Go your way. Forget her.'

'Do you think me so inconsistent?' the young man demanded. 'No, my nature is such that, while I am perfectly aware of the absurdity of this "passion," I do not suffer less.'

'Lord Ewald,' the professor remarked finally, 'you amaze me. You are one of England's richest and most distinguished peers. In your country there are many beautiful, eligible young women.

'You are a brilliant match, and you can certainly find some innocent, ideal girl whose love could only be given once in a lifetime. You could have a wonderful, happy future with such a wife.

'But here you are, shorn of your strength before this co-quette. It is absurd!'

'Come, my friend, don't be so hard on me,' Lord Ewald pleaded. 'I have taken myself to task very severely, but it is no use.'

'Yes,' said the elder man, 'but I am now speaking for the young girl who will be your salvation. You have a great deal to accomplish in this world, and she will be at your side to help and comfort you.'

The young nobleman shook his head sadly.

'Yes,' the professor continued as though to himself, 'it is serious, very serious – very grave indeed.'

Then, after a longer pause, he announced:

'Lord Ewald, I am, perhaps, the only physician under heaven who can help you! Now, I want you, for the last time, to give me a reply in a definite fashion:

'Can you not consider this affair merely as a gallant intrigue, as a romantic adventure? Any other man but you would. Can't you consider it as a worldly fancy, intense, if you wish, but of no vital importance?'

'It is impossible,' declared the young man. 'Miss Cleary might tomorrow be the love of but a day to many others – it is quite possible. But I can never change.

'I come of a race that loves only once, and, when we fail, we disappear quietly. The shadings and concessions we leave to others. There is no other form of beauty but hers in this life for me.'

'But, despising her as you do, why do you persist in exalting this point of beauty, if you say that your desires have become forever contemplative and frozen?'

'That is very true. I have no desire for her. But she has become the radiant obsession of my mind.'

'Do you absolutely refuse to take up your social life again?' inquired the professor.

'Absolutely,' replied Lord Ewald, as correct and calm as always, he took up his hat.

His host arose also.

'My dear boy,' he said, 'do you suppose for an instant that I am going to sit calmly by and let you walk out of here to blow out your brains, without making an effort to save you? You saved my life. I owe mine and all that has come into it to what you have done for me. Do you think that I have been questioning you without a motive?

'My dear fellow, you are one of those sick persons who can only be treated with poison, so I have determined, since all other remonstrances are useless, to doctor you thus, if you will permit me. It will be in a terrible way, as your case is an exceptional one. The remedy consists of enabling you to realize your dreams.

'Great heavens! It seems to me now that, unconsciously, I

have expected you this evening. Now, I see it. Yes, your dreams shall be realized!

'There are wounds that cannot be cured except by probing deeper into them. I am going to accomplish your dreams in their entirety. When you spoke of Alicia Cleary, did you not utter these words:

' "*Who could put a soul into that body!*" '

'Yes,' murmured the young nobleman.

'I can!' exclaimed the professor. 'I shall put a wonderful soul into that beautiful body!'

V.

'My lord,' said Professor X, speaking with the solemnity of a great physician, 'do not forget that in carrying out your singular wish I agree to do so only out of necessity.'

The strange tone and the look which accompanied it made Lord Ewald start. A slight tremor of premonition passed over him. He glanced keenly at his host, wondering if he was in possession of his faculties, for the words that he had just uttered passed all intelligence.

But, in spite of this feeling, an irresistible magnetism had come from the professor's last words. The young Englishman had a presentiment of an imminent miracle.

Taking his gaze from the inventor's face, his glance travelled over the various objects strewn about. Under the brilliant light given off by the lamps these marvels of scientific discovery assumed disturbing configurations. The laboratory took on the appearance of a magic grotto.

Lord Ewald was aware that most of his host's discoveries were still unknown to the world. The professor's real character, constantly paradoxical to his reputation, surrounded him, in Lord Ewald's eyes, with an intellectual halo, as he stood in the centre of the wonders to which he belonged. To the young guest his host was like the inhabitant of a superelectrical, a supernatural, realm.

After a few moments he felt himself won over by a blending of sentiments, curiosity and amazement, and with these there was a new feeling, a new *hope*. The vitality of his being was augmented.

'You seem amazed,' the professor remarked. 'It is merely a matter of transsubstantiation. I have already made some tests, and I am well satisfied with my experiments so far.'

He paused a moment, and then demanded brusquely:

'Do you accept the proposition?'

'Are you speaking seriously?' Lord Ewald countered.

'Certainly!'

'Then I'll give you *carte blanche*,' said Lord Ewald, with a sad little smile, which was, however, already a trifle worldly.

'Very well,' said the professor, glancing at the electric clock which hung over the door, 'I will commence, then, for time is precious, and I need three weeks.

'It is now eight thirty-five. Twenty-one days from now, at this same hour, Alicia Cleary will stand before you, not only transformed, not merely a delightful companion, with a mind of the highest intellectual type, but reclothed in a phase of immortality.

'In fact, this dazzling creature will no longer be a woman, but an angel – not only a woman, but the beloved – not the cold Reality, but the Ideal.'

'What an extraordinary statement!' his lordship exclaimed.

'Oh, I will show you how it will be brought about,' said the professor. 'The result will be so marvellous in itself that the apparent disillusions of its scientific analysis will fade away before the sudden and profound splendour of the achievement.

'So, if only to reassure you that I am absolutely sane, and that I am in full possession of my faculties, for I can see from your look that you have your doubts upon this matter, I will take you into my secret this very evening.

'But we must get back to work right now. Where is Miss Cleary now?'

'At the opera.'

'What is the number of her box?'

'Number seven.'

'Did you tell her that you were coming down here to see me alone this evening?'

'No. It would have been of such small interest to her that I did not think it necessary.'

'Has she ever heard of my name?'

'Perhaps, but she would have forgotten it.'

'So much the better – that is important.'

While he was speaking the professor walked over to the phonograph, which was connected to the telephone. Glancing for a moment at the record, he adjusted the needle to a certain spot and started the instrument.

'Are you there, Martin?' the instrument cried out with the professor's voice.

There was no reply.

'I bet the rogue has thrown himself down on my lounge and gone to sleep,' remarked the scientist, smilingly.

Shutting off the machine, he took up the receiver of a perfected microphone, adjusted it to the ear, and observed:

'Ah, it is just as I thought. He has had his nightcap and has gone to sleep. He is snoring loudly enough.'

'Where is this person to whom you wish to speak?' inquired Lord Ewald.

'He is in my office in the city – about twenty-five miles from here.'

'And you can hear a person snoring at that distance?'

'If he snored like this fellow,' said the professor, laughing, 'I could hear him at the North Pole. Strange, isn't it? If you were to tell a fairy story like that to a child, it would say: "That is impossible," and yet it is possible.

'In the near future, no one will be astonished to hear voices and sound from a great distance. I predict this. Now, I am going to give this fellow something that will tickle him.'

As he spoke, he applied the hooded mouthpiece of another piece of apparatus to the transmitter of the telephone.

'Let us hope that this won't scare the horses on the street,' he muttered as he set it in motion.

'Are you there, Martin?' the instrument shouted.

A few seconds later there was heard the deep voice which had spoken to the professor some time before, but which now was startled and evidently coming from a man who had been suddenly awakened from a sound sleep. The tones seemed to come from out of the hat which Lord Ewald held in his hand, which had by chance come in contact with a condensator that was suspended near by.

'What is wrong?' cried the voice. 'Is there a fire?'

'There!' exclaimed the professor. 'I got him to his feet quick enough.'

Then, going over to the telephone into which he had spoken before, he said:

'Don't be alarmed, Martin: just a false alarm to awaken you. The warning is only set at eighteen degrees. I am sending you a message which I want you to get off at once by hand.'

'Very well, sir. I am ready.'

The professor tapped off a message in code on the dial plate of a Morse instrument.

'Have you read it?' he asked.

'Yes, sir,' the voice answered. 'I'll take it myself.'

Whether by accident or by a jocular design on the part of the inventor, who had placed his hand on the central control of the laboratory, the voice appeared to rebound from corner to corner on all sides of the immense room. It appeared as if a dozen individuals, faithful echoes of one another, were all speaking at the same time.

'And, Martin,' added the professor, 'let me have the reply quickly.

'That is settled,' he said, turning round to face Lord Ewald. 'All goes well.'

Then his whole manner changed. He looked at the young man fixedly, and in a tone that was impressive, he declared:

'My lord, I now have to inform you that we are going to leave the domains of normal life. Together we are to enter a world of phenomena which are as unusual as they are impressive.

'I will endeavour to present you with a key to the riddle. At first we are going to verify – nothing more. You are going to be shown a being, a vision of indefinite mentality. Although her aspect will be familiar, the sight of this being will be enough to give you a great shock.

'You will run no physical risks. However, I feel that it is my duty to warn you that you will need all your coolness, and perhaps much courage, to support you at the first sight of the marvel.'

Lord Ewald regarded the scientist closely, hesitatingly. Then, after a brief pause, he replied:

'Thanks for your warning. I hope that I shall be able to control myself. Let us proceed.'

The professor now became very energetic. Going over to the big French windows, he closed them, drawing together the inside shutters and fastening them securely. He then crossed hurriedly to the door leading from the laboratory and pushed the bolt.

This done, he closed the switch of a danger signal which flashed an intense red light above the laboratory, giving warning to those at a distance that a dangerous experiment was being conducted, and that any one who came near the laboratory was doing so at the risk of his life.

Raising a lever, he disconnected all of the micro-telephonic inductors, with the exception of the call bell, which connected the laboratory with the city office.

'Now,' said the scientist, 'we are almost cut off from the world of the living.'

Seating himself at his table full of telegraphic apparatus, he began to arrange several wires with his left hand while with his right he seemed to be tracing some strange characters, his lips moving constantly, as if he were murmuring some weird incantation.

'Haven't you a picture of Miss Cleary on you?' he asked, continuing to write.

'Oh, yes,' replied Lord Ewald. 'I forgot. I might have shown it to you.'

Taking a small picture from his pocket, he handed it to the professor, saying:

'Here she is – in all her statuesque beauty. Look and see for yourself that I have not exaggerated.'

The professor took the photograph and looked at it.

'She is marvellous!' he exclaimed. 'Here certainly is the famous Venus of the sculptor. The resemblance is amazing. You are quite right, she is the Venus de Milo come to life.'

He turned and touched the regulator of a battery near at hand. Immediately there was a flash, as a flaming electrical arc jumped across the huge points of a double wire of platinum. With a sizzling crackle it flickered for several seconds, as though it were searching on all sides for a means of escape.

A blue wire, one end of which was grounded, was near by. The questing arc seized upon it and disappeared.

An instant later a sombre, rumbling noise was heard underneath the feet of the two men. It rolled onward, as though it were coming from the bowels of the earth, or indeed from the profound depths of an abyss. One might have thought that ghostly phantoms were shattering a glacial sepulchre and dragging its long-lost occupant back to the surface of the earth.

The scientist, still holding in his hand the photograph, had his eyes fixed on a point in the wall at the other end of the laboratory. His attitude was tense.

The noise, which had continued to ascend in a crescendo, suddenly ceased.

The hand of the master engineer pressed an ebony lever on the table.

'*Hadaly!*' he called, as if he were summoning some one to appear from the spirit world.

VI.

As the professor called out this mysterious name, a section of the wall at the extreme south of the laboratory turned on its hinges, silently bringing to view a narrow retreat fashioned between the slabs of stone. All the light from the electrical globes was suddenly focused on this spot.

The concave and semicircular walls were covered with rich draperies of black velvet, which fell luxuriously from an arch of jade to the white marble floor. The heavy folds were hooked back and fastened by retainers of gold, caught here and there through the rich material.

On a dais in the centre of this niche was standing a being whose aspect bore the impression of the Unknown.

The vision appeared to have a face of shadows, phantom-like. In the centre of the forehead a network of pearls caught together and held in place folds of black gauze which completely hid the rest of the head. A suit of armour, fashioned of leaves of burned silver, which were moulded with a myriad of perfect shadings, covered her girlish form.

The front of the black veil crossed over under the round metal collar, and was then thrown over the shoulders and knotted at the back of the head. The flimsy lengths of this veil fell to the waist of the apparition like a cloud of hair and then blended to the floor with the dark shadows of her presence.

A draping of black batiste was drawn around the hips and tied before her. The long black fringes of the drapery which fell behind her appeared to be sewn with sparkling brilliants. Between the folds of her belt could be seen the gleam of a naked weapon of oblique form.

The phantom leaned her right hand on the hilt of this blade while in her left hand, which hung down beside her, she held an everlasting flower of gold. On every finger of her hands sparkled rings set with precious stones, and these circlets in turn were fastened on the delicate gauntlet on her hand.

The mysterious being, after standing motionless for a few moments, descended the one step from the dais, and came forward, towards the two men.

Although her footsteps appeared soft, they resounded throughout the laboratory as she advanced, the powerful lights playing on her gleaming armour.

The vision advanced until it was within three steps of the professor and his guest. Then, in a voice that was exquisitely grave, the apparition said:

'My dear master, I am here.'

Lord Ewald gazed in nervous wonderment at this extraordinary sight.

'The hour has come for you to live, Hadaly,' said the great

electrician.

'Ah, master, I do not wish to live,' murmured the soft voice through the hanging veil.

'But this young man has come here to accept life for you,' the inventor explained as he threw into a jade vase the photograph of Alicia Cleary which he had been holding in his hand.

'Then,' said the vision resignedly, after a moment's pause, and with a slight inclination of her head towards Lord Ewald, 'let it be according to his wish.'

When the vision uttered these words the inventor, by regulating the claws of a circuit breaker, caused a sponge of magnesium at the other end of the laboratory to burst into a brilliant flame.

A powerful, pencil-like ray of dazzling light shot forth, directed by a reflector, and this ray was in turn reflected onto an object glass adjusted opposite the photograph of Alicia Cleary. Another reflector, placed above the photograph, multiplied the refraction of the penetrating rays upon it.

Almost instantaneously a square of glass, placed in the centre of the object glass, became tinted. Then the square of glass appeared to lift itself from out of its groove in the object glass and to enter into a metallic cell which had two circular openings.

The incandescent rays entered through one of these openings, passing through the tinted glass in the centre, and came forth on the opposite side, which surrounded the wide cone of a projector.

Immediately, in a large frame on a sheet of white silk stretched on the wall, there appeared, life-size, the luminous and transparent image of a young woman – the blood and flesh and bone statue of the Venus de Milo in truth, if such one ever breathed in this world of illusions.

'I am dreaming!' exclaimed Lord Ewald in bewilderment.

'Hadaly,' said the scientist, 'that is the form in which you will be incarnated!'

The vision took a step toward the radiant image, which she appeared to contemplate for a moment from behind the darkness of her veil. Then she murmured in a soft voice, as if to herself:

'Oh, so beautiful – and to force me to live!'

And bowing her head on her chest with a deep sigh, she whispered:

'So be it!'

The magnesium went out. The vision in the frame disappeared.

Before the spell of emotion which this picture caused had been dispelled, the professor raised his hands to the height of the vision's forehead. She trembled a little, then, without a word, she offered the symbolic golden flower to Lord Ewald, who could not repress a faint chill when he accepted it.

Turning to one side, the phantom began the same somnambulistic walk back to the mysterious regions whence she had come. When she reached the threshold she turned, and, raising her two hands towards the black veil over her face, she threw, with a charming gesture, a kiss to the professor and his guest.

Then she entered the opening, lifted a fold of one of the black draperies, and disappeared from view.

The wall closed again. There was the same sombre, rumbling noise that was heard before, but this time it seemed to be descending and dying away into the bowels of the earth. It stopped as suddenly as it had begun. The two men were again alone under the bright lights of the laboratory.

'Who is this strange being?' Lord Ewald demanded, half fearfully, placing in his lapel the emblematic flower that Hadaly had given to him.

The professor fixed his gaze on Lord Ewald's face as he replied calmly:

'It is not a living being!'

At these words the younger man also stared in turn at the scientist, as if demanding whether he had heard rightly.

'Yes,' the professor continued, replying to the unspoken question in the young man's eyes, 'I affirm that this form which walks, speaks, and obeys, is not a person or a being in the ordinary sense of the word.'

Then, as Lord Ewald still looked at him in silence, he went on:

'At present it is not an entity; it is no one at all! Hadaly, externally, is nothing but an electro-magnetic thing – a being of limbo – a possibility.

'Presently, if you wish, I will unveil to you the secret of her magic nature. But here is something that will give you enlightenment.'

VII.

He guided the young man through the maze of miscellaneous instruments installed about the room before they stood before the ebony table.

'What impression do you get at sight of that?' he asked, pointing to the whites-kinned feminine hand and arm lying on the violet silk cushion.

Lord Ewald gazed with a still greater thrill of astonishment at the unexpected human relic on which the light from the marvellous lamps now focused.

'What is it?' he asked.

'Look at it well,' the professor urged, evasively. 'Examine it.'

The young man leaned over. He lifted up the hand, then he drew back abruptly and demanded:

'What can it mean – a human hand – and it is still warm?'

'Don't you find anything extraordinary in the arm?' the professor inquired.

Lord Ewald resumed his examination for a moment, and exclaimed:

'Good heavens, this is as great a marvel as the phantom.

If it had not been for the excision here, I could not have seen that it was a masterpiece of scientific skill.'

The young Englishman appeared to be fascinated by the object. He took up the arm and began comparing his own hand with the feminine fingers.

'The weight – the form – the colour, even,' he murmured, as if in a stupor. 'Do you mean to tell me that this is not human flesh that I am touching at this moment? Upon my word, my own hand trembles at the very touch of it.'

'That is better than human flesh,' said the scientist simply. 'Human flesh fades and grows old. Here is a composition of delicate substances compounded by chemistry in such a way as might well confuse nature herself.

'But let us say this is a copy of nature – to use this word empirically – which will always appear living and young. A thunderbolt could destroy it, but it will never age. It is artificial flesh, and I can explain how it is produced. You have only to read Berthelot.'

The younger man could only murmur in stupefaction:

'Eh? What did you say?'

'I say that it is artificial flesh,' declared the professor. 'I believe that I am the only one who can fabricate it to such perfection.'

Lord Ewald, who was now in such a state of confusion that he could not readily express his thoughts, again turned to examine the artificial arm.

'But, professor,' he said, 'this pearly fluid – this carnal splendour and the intense life in it – how was it possible to produce such an amazing illusion?'

'Oh, that part of the experiment is a mere nothing. It is done simply by the aid of the sun,' was the smiling response.

'In a certain sense, we can catch the secret of the sun's vibrations, and once the shade of the dermal whiteness is determined I reproduce it by a setting of the object plates.

'Here is how I do that,' he continued. 'Albumin is supple, but it solidifies; the elasticity in this example is due to hydraulic pressure. This material is then made sensitive by a very subtle photochromatic action. Of course, I had a splendid model.

'As for the rest, it is simple; the humerus constructed of ivory contains a galvanic marrow in constant communication with a network of induction wires which are entwined in the same way as nerves and veins, and which are held between the releases of a perpetual calorific unit that gives to it this impression of warmth and malleability.

'If you wish to know where the elements of this network are disposed, how they feed themselves, so to speak, and in what manner the static fluid transforms its action into almost animal heat, I can give you the entire anatomy of it. It is nothing more than a matter of handwork.

'What you see here is an Andraiad of my making, moulded for the first time by the amazing vital agent we call electricity. This gives to my creation the blending, the softness, and the illusion of life.'

'An Andraiad?'

'Yes,' said the professor, 'a human-imitation, if you prefer that phrase. In the future we will have to be careful that the facsimile does not, in the manufacture, surpass the model physically. That is a danger to be avoided.

'I suppose, my dear fellow, that you know the kind of mechanism that has heretofore been employed in the attempt to forge a human image.'

Lord Ewald nodded.

'But,' the professor remarked, with a scornful laugh, 'they tried to work without the proper means of execution – and what was the result? They simply produced monsters – scarecrows for birds.

'These anatomies were only fit for a place in the most hideous waxwork shows, wretched objects that exude a strong odour of wood, rancid oil, and gutta percha. Such false sycophants, instead of giving man a knowledge of his power, could only make him bow his head before the god Chaos.

'You know their jerky and irregular movements, their absurdity of line and colour, the frightful wigs they wore, the noise of their mechanism, their stiffness, and the sensation of emptiness which they created. They were all just horrible masks, all caricatures of our race. Such were the first models of Andraiads.'

The face of the inventor grew severe, his voice became didactic and hard.

'But, to-day,' he went on, 'that time has passed. Scientific discoveries have multiplied. Metaphysical conceptions are refined. Instruments of counterdraw are so accurate, so precise, and so dependable that man is now able to attempt far greater things than formerly.

'We now are able to realize the powerful phantoms of mixed-presences of which our predecessors could never have even conceived an idea. They would have ridiculed the idea and declared it impossible.

'Just now, for instance, when you saw Hadaly, it would have been almost impossible for you to have smiled at her aspect. But, I assure you, that so far she is only a rough diamond. She is only the skeleton of a shadow waiting for the shadow to appear.

'Is it not true that you received the same sensation in touching the limb of that Andraiad that you would have received in touching the limb of a human being?'

Lord Ewald nodded.

'Well, now,' said the professor, 'just make another test. Will you clasp that hand? Perhaps it will return the pressure!'

Lord Ewald took the slim fingers in his and pressed them slightly.

He gasped in amazement. The hand responded to his pressure in an affable manner, so soft and sweet, yet seemingly so far off that he thought it must be a part of an invisible body. With an uncanny feeling he let the shadowy object drop hastily.

'Ghostly!' he exclaimed.

The inventor smiled at the young man's amazement.

'That is nothing,' he said, 'in comparison to what can be done. Oh, this great work – this creation – if you only knew – if you –'

The professor stopped short, as if a sudden, new idea had come to him – an idea so terrible that it cut short his speech.

'Truly,' cried Lord Ewald, with a forced laugh, 'I feel as though I were in the presence of some mighty wizard of the middle ages. What are you thinking of now, professor?'

The great inventor remained silent for a few moments, immersed in deep thought. Then he sat down and looked with a new anxiety at the young man who stood before him.

'My lord,' he said finally, 'I have just perceived that, with a young man of your imagination, an experiment might lead to fatal results! I am dubious.

'Hearken! When one stands on the threshold of a blacksmith's shop he sees a man working in the smoke, a fire, and implements. The anvil rings out as the smith fashions bars, blades, tools.

'But the man who is making these things is entirely ignorant of the unexpected usage to which his products will be put. He can only call them by their common names. And that is true with all of us.

'No blacksmith can estimate correctly the true nature of the object he is forging, for the simple reason that all knives may become daggers and do murder. It is the usage that one makes of a thing which re-baptizes and transforms it.

'Our uncertainty of the ultimate use of an object alone makes us irresponsible. Therefore, if one would dare to accomplish anything, he must know how to properly safeguard it.

'The mechanic who melts lead into the form of a bullet says unconsciously, "This is thrown to chance, perhaps it is lost," and he finishes this messenger of death, the soul of which is veiled from his eyes.

'But if the gaping, mortal wound that his bullet is destined to make could, by chance, be made to pass before his eyes, the mould for the bullet would drop from his hands, if he were an honest man. No doubt he would refuse bread for his children's meal, if that bread could only be bought at the price of the achievement of his task. He would hesitate, for he would feel himself to be, of a certainty, an accomplice of a future homicide –'

'Yes, that is true,' Lord Ewald interrupted; 'but how does this concern you, professor? You are not making bullets.'

'But I am in the position of that workman,' was the grave response. 'I am fashioning heated metal on the forge, and just now, in thinking of your temperament and your disillusions, I seemed to see the wound before my eyes.

'This is what troubles me: the thing about which I want to speak to you might be good for you, while, on the other hand, it might prove more fatal to you than a mortal wound. So, I hesitate.

'We are both going to take part in an experiment which may, in reality, prove more dangerous for you than it at first appears. A most horrible peril will menace you, and you are certainly already in a dangerous mood, since yours is the nature that a fatal passion almost always leads to a desperate end.

'I know, on the other hand, that there is a great chance that I can save you. But if the cure is not what I expect, it will be far better to remain as you are.'

'Since you speak in such a serious manner,' said Lord Ewald, with an effort, 'I can only tell you one thing: I intended to put an end to my intolerable existence this very night!'

The professor gazed at the young man in consternation.

'To-night!' he exclaimed.

'Yes. So, you see, you need hesitate no longer on my account,' affirmed Lord Ewald quietly.

'The die is cast,' murmured the professor to himself. 'Who would have thought it – he is to be the one!'

'Again I ask you to be good enough to tell me what you are hinting,' said Lord Ewald.

A deep silence followed, and in that pause it seemed to Lord Ewald that he could feel the breath of the Infinite pass swiftly over his forehead.

'Then,' cried the inventor, drawing himself up to his full height, his eyes blazing, and his speech becoming rapid and assured, 'since I feel myself defied in this manner by the Unknown – so be it!

'Here is what I am driving at, my lord. I am going to realize for you what no man has dared to attempt for another. I owe my life and all that I have to you, and I seize this opportunity to show you my great gratitude.

'You say that your happiness, your very being, is held prisoner by a human presence – the presence only. You are held prisoner in the glory of a smile, the beauty of a face, the sweetness of a voice.

'A living being has brought you to this, her unusual attractions have brought you to the very threshold of death. I shall remake her own image and presence.

'I will show you, immediately, in a cold and calculating

manner perhaps, but indisputably, how, with the actual and formidable resources of science, I can reproduce the grace of her movements, the ring of her voice, the perfume of her flesh, the lines of her form, and the light of her eyes.

'I will show you the spring of her step, her carriage, her personality, her facial expression, her features, even her shadow, the reflection of her identity, on the ground. I will destroy her insipid animality. I will annihilate her selfish frivolity.

'At first I will reincarnate all this exterior, which is so exquisitely vital to you, in an apparition whose resemblance will far surpass your hopes and all your dreams.

'Then, finally, in place of the soul, which so repels you in this living woman, I will instil another soul, less conscious of itself, perhaps – and yet, how do we know that it will be, and what does that matter? – but suggestive of impressions a thousand times more beautiful, more noble, more elevated, a soul reclothed in its character of eternity, without which life is but a comedy.

'I will duplicate this woman with the sublime aid of light. And, projecting it on her radiant matter, I will illuminate from your idealized melancholy the imaginary soul of this new woman who will be capable of astounding even the angels.

'I will bring the illusion down to earth. I will imprison it. I will force into this phantom your ideal. You shall be the first to gaze upon her, for she will be your ideal woman, palpable, audible, materialized.

'I will seize, at the height of its sublimity, the first hour of this enchanted mirage which you follow in vain. I will seize it and enshrine it securely, almost immortally, in the one and only form where you have seen it. I will duplicate the living woman and fashion her new being according to your desires.

'I will give to this spirit all the songs of Antonio, of Hoffman; all the passionate mysticism of Poe's Lygeia; all the ardent seductions of the Venus of that master musician, Wagner! I will prove in advance that I can positively bring through human science a being made in our own likeness, out of the mire of actuality – a creation which, consequently, will be the same in effect as if it were actually created by nature.'

The great engineer, the light of genius shining in his eyes as he uttered these words, raised his hand in a solemn oath.

VIII.

Lord Ewald turned pale. The proposition that the great physician had just made was so astounding, so fantastic, that he was not sure that he had understood him, or that he wished to understand him. After a stupefied pause he murmured, for lack of anything decisive to say:

'But such a creature would be an insensible doll, with no intelligence whatever!'

'My lord,' declared the professor gravely, 'I swear that I can do what I have promised. You must be on your guard that in the juxtaposition of this Andraiad and the living model, and in listening to them both, you do not mistake the one for the other; that you do not believe the living woman to be the doll.'

A faint, scornful smile played about Lord Ewald's lips as he recalled Alicia Cleary's unmistakable, empty, frivolous mannerisms, but he forced himself to reply politely:

'Your conception is indeed prodigious, professor – but let us say no more about it. The work would always smell of the mechanism. You will excuse my smiling, dear friend, but you cannot *make* a woman. I wonder, as I listen to you, if your genius –'

'One moment,' interrupted the professor calmly. 'I swear to you that, at first, you will not be able to tell one from the other, and again I assure you that I am now in a position to prove my assertions.'

'Impossible!' Lord Ewald asserted.

'Again, for the third time, I pledge you my word to furnish you presently, no matter how little you desire it, with the most positive demonstration, not of the possibility of the fact, but of its mathematical certitude.'

Lord Ewald, still incredulous, exclaimed: 'You, born of a woman – you can reproduce the identity of a woman!'

'Certainly – and what is more, the reproduction will be more identical than the woman herself, for there is not a day that passes without bringing some change to the human form, even altering some lines.

'Physiology shows us that our body renews its atoms entirely every seven years. That being true, how can one ever wholly resemble oneself?

'This young lady about whom we are speaking, and you and I – we have all changed, all aged one hour and twenty minutes, since we began our discussion this evening.'

'You say that you will reproduce her in all her beauty, her voice, her walk – her exact appearance, in fact?'

'Positively. I will do it with electromagnetism and radiant matter. I could even deceive a mother, so I am sure that I can fool a lover.

'I will duplicate Miss Cleary in such a way that if in a dozen years from now she should look upon her idealized double, who will have remained unchanged, she could only do so with tears of envy – and terror.'

There was a pause.

'But,' murmured Lord Ewald thoughtfully, 'to undertake the creation of such a being seems to me sacrilegious.'

'The matter is entirely in your hands,' said the inventor simply.

'But could you put a sort of intelligence in this being?'

'I will give her intelligence itself.'

This impressive declaration fairly stunned Lord Ewald. He stood before the inventor as if petrified. They stared at each other silently.

A desperate game had been proposed, and the stakes were a spirit.

Lord Ewald broke the silence with a rallying laugh.

'A wonderful dream, my dear genius,' he said, 'a very wonderful dream. I see that you have great faith in the outcome, but it is a dream that is as frightful as it is impossible.

'However, dear friend, your sympathy and your desire to help me have touched me deeply. I cannot thank you enough.'

'My dear fellow,' the professor protested, 'I can see that

you secretly feel that it is not an impossible dream, for you hesitate!'

Lord Ewald wiped the beads of perspiration from his brow.

'I don't believe that Miss Cleary would ever consent to it,' he said, 'and, I admit, I would hesitate myself to let her do so.'

'That part of the problem concerns me only,' his host declared. 'I give you my word that your dear friend will suffer in no way. My work would be incomplete otherwise.'

'Well, how about me?' Lord Ewald demanded. 'Do I not count for something in my love for her?'

'Yes, certainly, and you will count for something much more than you could ever imagine.'

'Yes, but do you suppose for a moment that you will be able to convince me of the reality of this new Eve, even if you do succeed? What formidable subtleties will you employ to do that?'

'Oh, that is merely a question of immediate impression where reason enters only as a secondary adjunct. Does one ever reason with the charm to which one submits? But, just wait – the presence of the vision, of the phantom coming to life, will answer your question for you.'

'I suppose that I can dispute,' Lord Ewald suggested, dubiously, 'that I can put up an argument during the course of the experiment?'

'Certainly, and, mark you, if only one of your objections exists, just one, we will both agree to stop the experiment and go no farther.'

'I must warn you that I have very keen eyes.'

'Your eyes?' the professor remarked, smilingly. 'Tell me, can you clearly see this drop of water? Yet, if I place it between these two sheets of crystal and then place the pieces of crystal before the reflector of this solar microscope, and then submit it to the exact refraction which I threw on to the white sheet over there, where you beheld your fascinating Alicia, you would be no less astounded at what you would see revealed than you were when you beheld her picture transplanted there.

'If we were to think of all the indefinite, the occult realities, which this liquid drop conceals we should understand that the power of our eyes, which is only a sort of a visible crutch, is insignificant. The relative difference between what we discover under the microscope and what we see without its help is almost infinite.

'And, in turn, we may well surmise that what we cannot discover with its magnifying aid is also beyond apprehension. Let us then remember that we can only see the things that suggest themselves to our eyes, and we can conceive of them only after we have beheld their mysterious entities.

'We only possess what we can feel according to our nature. Man, imprisoned in his moving self, struggles in vain to evade the illusion or to captivate his mocking senses.'

'In truth, my good Mr Wizard,' Lord Ewald observed, 'one would think that you seriously believe me capable of falling in love with your phantom.'

'If you were an ordinary person I should have that to fear. But your confessions have reassured me.

'Did you not say just now – did you not swear that your feelings for your beautiful, living friend were merely platonic? Well, then, you will only love Hadaly as she deserves, which is a far more beautiful sentiment than feeling an earthly love for her.'

'So you think I shall love her then?' demanded Lord Ewald, with a sceptical smile.

'Why not?' retorted the professor, in real surprise. 'Will she not be a perpetual incarnation in the only form where you can conceive love?'

'Yes, that is true. But one can only love an animated being. The soul is the unknown quantity.'

The professor smiled this time pityingly, but he made no comment on his lordship's dictum.

'Will the vision know who she is? I mean, what she is?' Lord Ewald persisted.

'Do you know so well yourself what you are? Do we know

what we are? Why, then, do you demand more of the copy than the Creator thought right to grant to the original?'

'Will this creature of your creation be able to feel any sentiment herself?'

'Without a doubt,' replied the professor, casually.

'Eh! What do you say?' cried Lord Ewald in amazement.

'Without a doubt,' the scientist repeated. 'This will depend entirely on you. It is upon you alone that I count for this phase of the miracle to be accomplished.'

'Well, then,' said Lord Ewald, 'be so kind as to inform me where I shall draw the spark of sacred fire which will enable us to achieve the spirit. My name is not Prometheus, but simply Ewald, and I am only mortal.'

'Nonsense,' replied the professor, 'each man is a Prometheus within himself without knowing it. My lord, I assure you that a single one of those divine sparks with which you have so often tried, in vain, to animate the negative personality of your adored one will suffice to put life into this shadow.'

'Prove it to me!' cried Lord Ewald. 'And perhaps –'

'As you will!' replied the professor. 'You have told me that the being that you love, and which, for you alone is real, does not exist in this human form, but only in your desires. This being then does not exist, or, better, you know that it does not exist. You have then neither been deceived by yourself nor by this woman.

'But, still, you close your eyes, rather the eyes of your spirit; and you close the demands of your conscience by seeking to find in this woman the phantom which you desire. Her true personality is to you the illusion which you seek, and which has been raised in your whole being by the brilliance of her beauty.

'It is this illusion alone which you try to bring forth, even to create, to call to life in the presence of your beloved, in spite of the incessant disillusionments which you suffer from this mortal – this frightful – this wretched emptiness of the real Alicia.

'It is then only a shadow that you are in love with, and it is for this shadow that you would die. It is this shadow that you would recognize absolutely as real.

'It is this vision conjured up by your desires, which you have called forth, which you have created in your living being, and this vision is nothing more than a double of your own soul which you have transplanted into her. Behold, then, your love is nothing else, you can plainly see, than a perpetual and always fruitless effort at redemption.'

For a few moments there was a profound silence between the two men.

'And now, then,' continued the professor, 'since it has been shown that it is only a shadow to which you have been lending so fictitiously and warmly a being, I am offering you a chance to try the same experiment upon a creature which will be a copy, externally realized, of your own shadow. It is an illusion for an illusion.

'The being of this mixed-presence, which we call Hadaly, will depend upon the free will of the person who will dare to conceive it. By "being," I mean soul.

'Why should you not be the one? Why should you not endeavour by means of your living faith to project some of your ideals into Hadaly in the same manner in which you strive to project them into your living friend?

'Try it. Breathe upon this ideal forehead of Hadaly and suggest to her your idealized being, and you will see how the Alicia of your dreams will be realized, unified, and animated in this phantom.

'Try it, if your last hope tells you so to do. And then, ask yourself in the depths of your conscience if this auxiliary phantom-creature, which shall draw forth in you anew the desire to live, is not truly more worthy to bear the name of a human being than the living one – the living one which has only given you the desire for death.'

Deeply perplexed, Lord Ewald murmured:

'Your deduction is truly most specific and profound, but I am sure that I should always feel somewhat alone when in the company of your unconscious Eve.'

'You will feel less alone with Hadaly than you will with

her model,' the professor announced. 'Besides, my lord, that will be your fault and not mine. One must feel that one is a superman before one dares to attempt what we have in question here.

'Besides all this, let us take into account the novelty of the impression that you will experience when you hold your first conversation with this Andraiad – this idealized Alicia – walking beside you with the sun's full rays falling upon her exquisite beauty, looking up at you with all the naturalness of the living woman.'

A smile spread over Lord Ewald's face.

'Ah, you doubt,' said the great electrician. 'You think that your senses would soon discover the change that I would substitute for nature. Well, then, listen to me: have you or Miss Cleary a dog?'

'Yes, she has a little black terrier that is devoted to her.'

'Good. Now, a dog has a keen scent – and I want you to make a wager with me.

'A dog could very easily recognize its mistress in the dark, even though she were in a crowd of a thousand persons. I will make you a bet that if we transform Hadaly into the living being, and have her call this dog, it will rush toward her and recognize her merely by the scent of her gown.

'I will even go farther than that. I will wager that if Miss Cleary and the phantom should call that dog simultaneously, that it would be the phantom, and the phantom only, that he will obey. Will you take the wager?'

'Haven't you stretched that point just a little bit?' asked Lord Ewald, greatly disconcerted.

'I only promise what I can perform,' stated the scientist briefly. 'The experiment has already been carried out most successfully. If, then, the scent of a lower animal, whose organs are superior to ours in keenness, can be deceived, why should I not dare to defy the control of the human senses?

'I want to say this,' the inventor went on; 'although Hadaly is a mystery, you must not look upon her in an exalted manner. Be natural with her. You must just think of her as being slightly more animated by electricity than her living model, that is all.'

'Why should she be more animated?'

'Well,' said the professor, 'have you ever seen a beautiful young brunette combing her hair before a large bluish mirror, in a room that has been darkened and in which the curtains are all drawn, on a stormy day? Have you ever seen the sparks fly out of her hair on the points of her tortoise-shell comb, like little diamonds sparkling on a black wave in the sea at night?

'But if you have never seen Miss Alicia like that, you can see Hadaly. Brunettes have a great deal of electricity.'

There was a pause.

'Are you agreed that we shall make the attempt at this incarnation?' asked the professor finally. 'Hadaly, in this golden flower, has offered to save you from the wreck of your love.'

'This is the most frightful proposition that was ever made to a desperate man,' Lord Ewald replied in almost a whisper, 'and yet, in spite of myself, I find the greatest difficulty in the world to take it seriously.'

'Seriousness will come,' declared Professor X; 'that is Hadaly's affair.'

'I suppose,' said his lordship, 'that any other man would accept this copy that you offer me very quickly, if only out of curiosity.'

'But I should not propose it to every man,' the inventor exclaimed, smiling. 'If I were to bequeath the formula to humanity there are those who would abuse the help that it is intended to give.'

'Could the experiment be suspended after it was started?'

'Yes, even after the work is completed, it can always be destroyed, if it seems the best thing to do.'

'But that would not be the same,' declared Lord Ewald. 'After it had been completed it would not be the same thing; one would feel as if a life were being taken.'

'Well,' said the scientist, 'remember that I am not urging or advising you in the slightest manner to accept this. You are suffering, and I have told you of a remedy. But the remedy is as dangerous as it is efficacious. You may refuse it – you are free to do so.'

Lord Ewald appeared still more perplexed.

'Oh, as to the danger,' he said with a shrug of his shoulders, 'you may forget that.'

'If it were only a physical danger,' said the professor, 'I would urge you to accept.'

'Do you think that it is my reason that is threatened?'

The professor did not answer at once.

'Lord Ewald,' he said at length, 'yours is the noblest nature that I have ever known. It was a very bad star that threw its light over you and led you to the realms of love. Your dreams have vanished, your wings have been clipped by a deceiving woman whose discordant nature constantly fans the flame of a sorrow that is consuming you, and which evidently will be fatal.

'Yes, you are one of the few remaining great lovers who would not deign to survive this sort of a test, in spite of the example of those all around you who are struggling against sickness, poverty, and love. You despise to become resigned to live under the lash of such a destiny.

'Your disease is in its worse stage. You told me just now that it is only a matter of hours. There is not even a doubt as to the issue of the crisis. It is obvious that when you go over the threshold of this house you are going to your death – your very bearing testifies to this.

'Now I am offering you life again; perhaps it will be at a great price, but who can tell the value of it at this moment? The ideal has lied to you. "Truth" has destroyed all desire. A woman has frozen the love in your heart.

'Why not say farewell to the pretended reality, the everlasting deceiver, and accept the artificial and its novel incitements that I offer you?

'If you would like to be the master of this situation, the dominator, let us make a pact. I will represent science with all its powerful mirages, while you – you shall represent humanity and its lost paradise.'

'Then choose for me,' said Lord Ewald calmly.

The professor was startled.

'That is impossible, my lord.'

'Well, then, what would you do in my place? If you had reached this state of mind that I am in, what would you do? Would you risk this absurd but disturbing adventure?'

The inventor looked at his young guest fixedly, his usually placid features twitching slightly, as if he had some secret thought that he could not express.

'I would not dare to express an opinion,' he said. 'I would have more of a motive in expressing one than most men.'

'Very well,' said Lord Ewald; 'which course would you choose if you had no alternative?'

'My lord,' said the professor gravely, 'do not doubt the deep attachment which I have for you, but with my hand on my heart –'

'What would you choose, professor?' his lordship persisted, inflexibly.

'Between death and the temptation in question?'

'Yes.'

The master electrician bowed to his guest. Then he said quietly:

'I would blow out my brains first.'

IX.

Lord Ewald made no reply for a moment. Then taking out his watch he glanced at the time and said, with a sigh:

'And now, this time we must part forever. I choose to die!'

The ringing of a bell was heard.

'You are a little late,' the professor announced. 'After your first words of resignation I commenced action.'

While speaking he started the phonograph, that spoke in his stead.

'Well?' cried its voice into the telephone.

The bass tones of the distant messenger were clearly audible in the laboratory. Their agitated intonations showed plainly that the speaker was somewhat out of breath.

'Miss Cleary was in box number seven at the opera. She will take the eleven-ten train,' said the messenger.

Lord Ewald, when he heard Miss Cleary's name shouted so boisterously and tensely, listened to the information.

'Very well,' he said, in cool acceptance of the pact, 'but what about getting back to the city? It will be very late.'

'Oh, I will attend to all that,' said the professor.

He placed a square of blank paper on the Morse receptor, which a few minutes later shot out of the frame.

'Here,' he remarked, calmly looking at the now printed sheet, 'is a charming little villa about twenty minutes from here. The lady who owns the place will expect Miss Cleary any time to-night.

'I can put you up here, but perhaps you would rather be near the villa. There is a very good inn close to it.'

'Oh, thanks very much,' said Lord Ewald, 'but I will go to the inn.'

'That's settled then,' continued the professor. 'Now I have this picture of Miss Cleary, and I will give it to my man and send him with the carriage to meet her train. He will easily recognize her from this. There will only be a few persons coming down at this hour, so you need not be anxious.'

While speaking he had taken a paste-board card from an object plate. He threw it into the receiver of a pneumatic tube after hurriedly writing a few words on the card.

The receiver corresponded with the transmitter of a pneumatic tube. In a moment a little bell, rung near by, announced that the order had been received and would be carried out.

Returning to the Morse apparatus, the professor continued to telegraph. When he had finished he turned suddenly to his guest and said:

'My lord, it goes without saying that it will be better not to speak to any one of this matter in which we are interested.'

'That is understood,' Lord Ewald said, simply. 'And I wish

to say, professor, that I no longer hesitate after accepting your proposition. Please consider this my final decision.'

The professor bowed his head gravely.

'Then I shall expect that your lordship will do me the honour to live twenty-one days. I also have a word to keep.'

'Agreed, but – not one day more,' said the young man stoically.

'I, myself, will offer you the pistol at nine o'clock in the evening of the day agreed upon, if I do not win your life,' Professor X agreed. 'And now, since we clearly understand each other, and are about to make a dangerous journey, I must kiss my children good-by.'

He took up the telephone transmitter and spoke two names into it.

The sound of a bell could be heard from the other side of the grounds.

'Here's a hundred kisses for you two,' said the inventor in a fatherly tone, as, with his mouth to the telephone, he sent a caress.

Then a strange thing happened.

Around these two men, searchers of the unknown – these two adventurers who were about to enter the realms of the shades, there suddenly broke out on all sides a vocal shower of kisses from the little children, who cried out in their sweet voices:

'Papa! Papa!' Send us some more!'

The professor had held the receiver gently against his cheek as it brought him the caresses.

When the good nights were over he turned to Lord Ewald and said:

'Now, my lord, I am ready.'

'No, professor,' the young man objected sadly, 'you must not go. I have no one dependent on me. It would be better for me to go alone on this trip, if it is possible.'

'We go together,' declared the engineer calmly.

Taking down two bear-skin coats from a panel in the wall, the professor handed one to his guest, saying:

'It is very cold where we are going. Wear this.'

Lord Ewald accepted the heavy coat and inquired:

'Would it be indiscreet for me to ask – to whose house are we going?'

'To Hadaly's, of course – in the midst of thunder, powerful electrical currents, and vast flashes of light.'

'Let us go then,' said the young man.

'Just a word. Before you go, have you no last questions, no last words that you would like to say to me?'

'No. Nothing. I must admit that I am rather in a hurry to have a talk with this pretty veiled creature whose nothing-ness has a call on my sympathy. As for the rest, the frivolous observations or questions which come to my mind, there will be always time –'

At these words the professor turned and stopped the younger man.

'Eh, what's that!' he cried. 'Do you forget, my dear fellow, that I call myself electricity, and that I, myself, have to struggle against your thoughts. If you have anything to say, you must speak at once.

'Tell me, now, of those frivolous anxieties and questions, or I shall not know what I am fighting against. It is not such an easy thing to match body for body with an ideal such as yours, I can tell you. Now, say all that you have to say to the physician who proposes to lighten your sorrow.'

'Oh, these ideas have no weight,' said Lord Ewald. 'They are just trivial thoughts on nothing.'

'Ah,' cried the professor, 'how you go on! "On nothing" – but a nothing can assume tremendous proportions! Who was it that said: "Not so long ago a kingdom was lost by the wave of a fan at the wrong moment. If Cleopatra's nose had been a trifle shorter, the face of the world would have changed"?

'Do you imagine that I do not appreciate the nothings? Now, if there is anything that makes you the least bit anxious, let us have it out. We will have it out before we start.

'We will go after you have told me, but let us begin, for we have only just time to make this visit and return before the living one arrives.'

'I wondered, first of all, why you questioned me so closely about the intellectual character of our feminine subject?' Lord Ewald explained.

'Because I was obliged to know what was the principal aspect under which you, yourself, conceived intelligence,' replied the engineer. 'The difficulty is in the physical reproduction. There is a question, at first, of imbuing Hadaly with the paradoxical beauty of your living subject.

'It is most important that the phantom, instead of disenchanting you as her model has, should be worthy in your eyes of the sublime form into which she will be incarnated. Unless we can do that it would not be worth while to make a change from the living to the phantom.'

'Very well. Now, how are you going to persuade Alicia to lend herself to this experiment?'

'This evening, when we are at supper, it will take me only a few minutes to persuade her to do what I want. You will see, even if I have to employ suggestions to decide her. But I am sure that I can persuade her.

'Then it will only be a matter of a few sittings, and a rough clay model will effect the change. She will not even see Hadaly, and she will not have the slightest knowledge of the work upon which we are engaged.

'Now, in order to incarnate Hadaly, to bring her forth from the almost supernatural atmosphere where the fiction of her identity is realized, this Valkyrie of science must be reclothed. If she is to come into our midst, she must have the fashions, the usage, and the aspect of the women of the present day?

'While the sittings are going on, dressmakers, glove-makers, lingerie-makers, corsetières, milliners, and bootmakers – I will give you the mineral substance for the insulation of the soles and the heels – will make exact copies of all the things worn by Miss Cleary, without her knowledge.

'These things will be given to her beautiful phantom as soon as she has come into the world. Once we have the measures all taken, you may have hundreds of duplicates made in different styles without its being necessary to try them on.

'It goes without saying that the Andraiad will use the same perfumes as her model, having, as I have said, the same emanations.'

'How will she travel?'

'Why, like any other person. There are travellers more strange than she. Hadaly, if warned of a voyage, will be quite irreproachable.

'She may be a little drowsy and irritable perhaps, speaking only at rare intervals and to you only, in a low voice, but she will be seated beside you and it will not be even necessary for her to lower her veil. She will defy all human observation.'

'Would she know how to act correctly if any one should address her?'

'In such a case you would simply have to state that the lady was a foreigner and did not know the language of the country. That would close the incident.

'In the matter of equilibrium even a good many living men and women have difficulty. Hadaly will not be able to take a rough sea voyage, but many men and women remain in their berths on a trip, because they become shaken by seasickness and look ridiculous.

'Hadaly's serenity should not be ruffled; she should not be humiliated by the sight of the defective organisms of her human companions. She will travel on sea in the same manner as a corpse.'

X.

'What; in a coffin?' cried Lord Ewald, aghast.

The professor nodded casually.

'Yes; in a coffin.'

'But not sewn up in a shroud, I hope?'

'No. This living object of art, not having known our bandages, will make her own winding sheet.

'This is how it will be done: Hadaly, among other treasures, possesses a heavy ebony casket, upholstered in black satin. The interior of this symbolic casket will be the exact mould of the feminine form that she is destined to take.

'This is her dowry. The upper sides of the casket open by the aid of a little gold key, in the form of a star, the lock of which is placed under the head of the sleeper.

'Hadaly knows how to enter this alone, either unclothed or entirely dressed. She lies down at full length and she knows how to arrange the linen sheets which are firmly attached to the interior in such a way that they do not even touch her shoulders.

'Her face is veiled; her head remains resting on a cushion; and around her brow is a band which helps to hold her in position. If it were not for her gentle, regular breathing, she would be taken for Miss Cleary, who had died that morning.

'On the closed door of this prison casket is nailed a plate inscribed with the name "Hadaly". This name signifies the ideal. The plate will be surmounted with your coat-of-arms, which will consecrate this captivity.

'The beautiful casket should be placed in a cedar case entirely lined with cotton wool. This should be square in shape in order not to arouse any suspicion. All of this will be ready in three weeks. On your return to London, a word to the director of customs will be all that is necessary to permit your mysterious luggage to enter.

'When Miss Cleary gets your last message of farewell, you will be in your castle at Athewold where you can awaken your heavenly vision.'

'In my castle,' murmured Lord Ewald, as if to himself, in a most profound and melancholy manner. 'Truly – there it will be possible.'

'Yes. There, in your solitary domain, surrounded by forests, lakes, and great rocks, you may in all security open Hadaly's prison. You have, I believe, in that castle some spacious rooms with furniture that dates back to the time of Elizabeth.'

'Yes,' agreed Lord Ewald, cynically, 'and I have enriched it with marvellous works of art. The old drawing room breathes the spirit of the genius of the past.

'The one great window in it is of stained glass draped with

hangings ornamented with floral garlands of burnished gold. It opens on to an iron balcony, the balustrade of which was wrought in the reign of Richard the Third. The moss-covered steps lead down to a long avenue of oak trees which extends the full length of the park.

'It is a beautiful place. Yes, this beautiful home was destined for my wife, if I could have met her.'

A shiver passed over him and he continued:

'What is to be, will be. I will take this illusory apparition, this galvanized hope, to my castle. As I am not capable to feel or have any desire for the other, I hope that this phantom form will brighten my days – my last dreams.'

'Good,' said the professor. 'I think that your castle will be just the place for this Andraiad. Hadaly will be like some mysterious somnambulist wandering around the lakes and over the heaths. In this far off castle where your old servants, your books, your hunting trophies, your paintings, and your musical instruments, are awaiting you, this newcomer will soon take her place.

'Respect and silence will make her stand surrounded in an isolated halo. The servants must receive orders from you never to speak to her. You can explain this by saying that having been saved, as by a miracle, from a terrific danger which threatened you, your companion had made a sacred vow never to speak to any one but you.

'There, in your castle, the beautiful voice which is so dear to you will sing to you the airs you love. You can accompany her on the organ, or with the soft note of the harp, or with the piano.

'Her exquisite notes will enhance the charm of the summer twilights, they will blend with the beauty of a sunlit day, and harmonize with the songs of the birds. In the autumn and in the winter nights her voice will rise above the sighing of the wind and the roar of the waves beating against the rocks.

'As she walks alone under the trees and through the old paths with her long gown trailing, a legend will soon be woven about her. The curious will have seen her strolling alone in the pale moonlight.

'She will be a terrifying sight, and none will know the secret but yourself.

'One day, perhaps, I shall come to visit you in your semisolitude where you have agreed to run two continual dangers – madness – and retribution.'

'You will be the only guest whom I shall receive,' declared Lord Ewald. 'But as only the preliminary possibility of this adventure is now established, let us see if the prodigy itself is possible. First of all, why is Hadaly enclosed in armour?'

'It is the plastic apparatus which is superimposed on the unity of the electric fluid that will correspond to the fleshy being of your ideal love. It contains, mounted within it, literally what corresponds to the interior organisms common to all human beings.'

'Will she always speak in the same low voice that I heard just now?'

'No. Decidedly not! She does not, even now, use that voice all of the time. Was Miss Cleary's voice always as it is now?

'Hadaly spoke, just now, in a soft, childish voice – spiritual, somnambulistic. No, she will have Miss Cleary's voice, just as she will have all her other attractions. Her singing voice and her speaking voice all remain, forever, just as it is indicated to her.

'In fabricating a woman, you must note, I have made use of the rarest and most precious substances, a compliment to the fascinating sex,' added the scientist gallantly. 'But I was obliged to use iron in the joints.'

'Ah! Isn't iron one of the constituents of our own bodies? Why have you used it only in the joints?'

'Because the force which holds the joints together is magnetic, produced by electrical currents. As iron is the metal which magnetizes and attracts best – it is much better than nickel or cobalt – I have used it in the form of steel.'

'But steel oxidizes. Won't her joints rust?'

'I have prepared against that. Here I have a large bottle of oil of roses, scented with amber. This is the lubricant for her joints.'

'Oil of roses?' queried Lord Ewald.

'Yes. It is the only one prepared in this manner that will always keep its exquisite aroma. Perfumes belong exclusively to the feminine world. Every month you will have to put a small spoonful of this oil in Hadaly's mouth while she is dozing.

'You see, it is all very human, just as if one were giving medicine to a child. The subtle perfume will diffuse in the magnetized metal organisms. This bottle will be sufficient for a century or more – and, my dear friend, I do not think that there will be any need for us to repeat the quantity!'

'You say that she will breathe?'

'Of course, the same as we do. But she will not burn oxygen as we do. We are chockful of it, like steam engines.

'Hadaly inhales and breathes air by the pneumatic movement of her chest which rises and falls like that of a woman in good health. The air, which passes between her lips and which makes her nostrils palpitate, is perfumed and warmed by electricity – an effluvia of amber and roses.

'The future Alicia's most natural attitude will be seated with her cheek on one hand and her elbow resting on something, or else reposing on a sofa, in the attitude of any graceful woman. She will maintain these attitudes without any other movement than her breathing.

'To awaken her from her phlegmatic existence, you will only have to take her hand. That will agitate the fluid in one of her rings.'

'One of her rings?' asked Lord Ewald, in surprise.

'Yes. The one on her forefinger. It is her wedding ring.'

Lord Ewald stared at the scientist in amazement.

'Do you know why that hand there responded to your pressure just now?' asked the professor, pointing to the object on the ebony table.

'No.'

'It was because, when you tightened your clasp, you pressed the ring. I don't know whether you have noticed it or not, but Hadaly has rings on all her fingers, and the various precious stones are sensitive.

'You need not bother her when she is in one of these extra-terrestrial attitudes; but if you wish to ask her anything you will be quite at liberty to do so.

'All you will have to do at a time like this, whether she is lying down on a couch or sitting up, is to take her hand and stroke the sympathetic amethyst in the ring on her forefinger, and she will get up gently, if you say to her: "Come, Hadaly." She will obey you better than the real woman.

'The touch of the ring should be slight and natural, as when you touch the hand of your living model. You may even do it with a slight fervour, in the interest of the illusion.

'Hadaly will walk straight before her and alone, at the request of the ruby which she wears on the middle finger of her right hand; or she will hold your arm and lean languishingly towards you; or she will follow wherever you wish to lead her, not merely as any woman would, but exactly as Miss Cleary would.

'You must not permit the fact that her human walk is controlled by means of these rings to shock you. Think how much more humiliating are the prayers and entreaties to which men have to resort, in order to bring the feminine graces to a semblance of obedience!

'In response to a persuasive touch on the turquoise on the ring finger, she will sit down, and in addition to these rings, she wears a three row necklace, each pearl of which has a corresponding action that will respond to its pressure.

'Here you have a fairly explicit manuscript – quite a conjuror's book – the most extraordinary ever seen, for it gives you a key to her habits and character. With a little practice – one must study women, you know – everything will become quite natural.'

The professor's gravity, as he made these statements, was quite imperturbable.

'Now,' he continued, 'about her food, she –'

'By Jove! Does she eat?' interrupted Lord Ewald.

'That seems to surprise you, my lord. Is it possible that you had contemplated, for a single instant, allowing this marvellous creature to die for lack of nourishment? Why, that would be worse than homicide.'

'But, pray, Mr Wizard, what do you mean by her food?' asked Lord Ewald. 'I must admit that, this time, you have gone beyond the most fantastic dreams.'

'Here is the nourishment that Hadaly must take two or three times a week,' said the professor. 'In this old chest I have some boxes of lozenges and certain tablets which she will assimilate very well. The strange girl will do it all alone. You will only have to place a dish on a stand or a table which will be always at a fixed distance from her habitual sleeping place, and indicate it to her by merely touching one of the pearls of her necklace.

'She will be quite a child in everyday, ordinary matters. She does not know, and you must teach her. We were all at that stage once, ourselves. But she will scarcely seem to remember – what of that, we, ourselves, often forget many things.

'She will sip from a thin goblet of jasper made especially for her. She will drink in precisely the same manner as her model. The goblet will be filled with filtered water.

'The lozenges are of zinc and the tablets are of bichromate of potassium, a few are of peroxide of lead. There is nothing strange in that. Nowadays, many of us take a variety of things which have been borrowed from chemistry.

'You will have to give her nothing more. She will not take any more than she will require. She will be very temperate. It would be a good thing if many of us would follow her example. But if she does not find her nourishment at hand when she needs it she will faint, or, rather, she will die.'

'She will die,' murmured Lord Ewald.

'Yes, so as to give her chosen one the divine pleasure of restoring her to life.'

'A very delicate attention,' said Lord Ewald, now smiling.

'Yes. When she remains motionless, with her eyes closed, you must restore her. All that you will have to do will be to give her a little clear water and a few of these tablets.

'But, as she will not have the strength to take them herself at such a time, you must touch the tourmaline on her middle finger – this stone communicates with a battery. That will be sufficient.

'As soon as she opens her eyes her first words will be to ask for water. Now, you must not forget to do this according to the directions given you in the manuscript. It is quite explicit.

'A few minutes after you have done this, our beautiful Hadaly will blow light fumes of pale smoke, faintly white in colour, from between her half closed lips, and then, there she is again living, as you and I, ready to obey all the rings and all the pearls, just the same as we accede to our own desires.'

'Do you mean to say that she blows clouds of smoke from her lips?'

'Just the same as we are continually doing,' said the professor, indicating the cigars which both he and his guest were holding. 'Only she does not hold an atom of metallic dust or smoke in her mouth. The fluid consumes and disappears in a moment. She has her cigarette, however, that is, if you –'

'I noticed that she has a dagger in her belt,' interrupted Lord Ewald.

'Yes. She would use that to defend herself if, while she is away from her chosen one, a trifler should dare to intrude upon her privacy. She would not tolerate the slightest familiarity. A blow from that dagger would be fatal. She is loyal to only one person, she will recognize one only – her master.'

'But she cannot see?'

'Who knows? Do we ourselves see very clearly? At any rate, she can guess or feel objects visible to you and me.

'Hadaly, I repeat, is a somewhat sombre young lady. She is indifferent to fate, and she would not hesitate to send a man to his death.'

'Then, a casual stranger could not take that weapon away from her?' asked Lord Ewald.

'I defy all the Hercules of the earth to do that,' declared the professor, laughing.

'How is that?'

'Because, enclosed in the dagger handle there is a most formidable power. A tiny opal on the little finger of the left hand connects the blade with a very powerful current. The carnelian alongside would deaden the noise of the electrical report.

'It is a veritable streak of lightning, so powerful that the first thoughtless fellow, who thought that he could steal a kiss from the sleeping beauty, would roll to the ground with his face blackened, and his limbs twisted, destroyed by the silent avenger. He would fall dead at Hadaly's feet before he had even time to touch her garment. She will certainly be a faithful, loyal friend.'

'I see,' Lord Ewald said. 'The kiss would form a conductor.'

'Here is a glass rod which has a beryl in it. This will neutralize the opal and, when you touch it with this, the dagger will drop, harmless. The formula for this tempered glass had been lost since the days of the Emperor Nero, but I found it.'

As he spoke, the professor struck the ebony table violently with the long gleaming switch of glass which had been lying near him. The radiant switch appeared to bend, but it did not break.

Then Lord Ewald asked, jokingly:

'Does she ever bathe?'

'Naturally – every day,' replied the professor, as if he were astonished at the question.

'But how does she do that?'

'Well, you know that all photochromatic proofs have to

remain in a specially prepared water for several hours. This strengthens them.

'The photo-chromatic action which I have mentioned is indelible; you understand that the skin is entirely saturated with it. It has been subjected to a process of light which gives it an impervious glaze.

'A small pink pearl on the left of the three-row necklace which Hadaly wears brings together an interior interposition of stones, the adherence of which hermetically prevents the water in the bath from penetrating the mechanism of this nymph. You will find the names of the perfumes in the manuscript which must be used in the baths.

'I will register the magnificent head of hair which Miss Cleary has upon the cylinder of movements. It will be reproduced exactly.'

'The cylinder of movements?' echoed Lord Ewald, questioningly.

'You will have to see it to understand. From what I have told you, you can apprehend that Hadaly, primarily, is a superb mechanical vision, almost a human being, a brilliant *facsimile*.

'The faults which I have given her out of courtesy to humanity consist only in that there are several types of woman in her – the same as there is in every woman. But the supreme type which dominates her is, if I may say it, perfect.

'She only plays the other types. She is a wonderful actress, with greater and even more serious talent than Miss Cleary.'

'And yet she is only a counterfeit being,' Lord Ewald remarked, with profound regret.

'Oh, as for that, the biggest minds have always wondered what the being in ourselves really is. Hegel, in his great work, says that the pure idea of the being, that is the difference between the being and nothingness, is only a simple matter of opinion. Hadaly herself will clearly resolve the question of her being, I can promise you.'

'How?'

'By words.'

'But if she is not a soul, will she have a conscience?' asked the younger man.

'Pardon me,' the professor said admonishingly, 'but isn't that precisely what you demanded? Didn't you cry out: "Who could put a soul into that body?"

'You have called for a vision precisely identical with your friend Alicia, without the conscience which has caused you so much sorrow. *Hadaly has come in answer to your call.* That is all.

'And I do not think that it will be a very great loss if Hadaly is lacking the kind of a conscience that her model has – do you? It will be to her advantage not to have it, at least, in your eyes, since Miss Cleary's conscience seems to be deplorable, a blot on the masterpiece. The conscience of a worldly woman – bah!'

'Even though a woman has caused me great sorrow,' Lord Ewald demurred gently. 'I think that you speak of the sex with much severity.'

XI.

Lord Ewald arose. He threw his bearskin coat over his arm, put on his hat and gloves, and adjusted his eyeglass. Then he said:

'It is useless to argue with you about a woman's conscience, my dear doctor. You would have a crushing reply for everything that I could say. I am ready to go on our little adventure when you are.'

'Then we will be off right now,' the professor agreed, rising briskly from his seat. 'One hour has already passed, and the train from the city will start in an hour. We have only an hour and a half for our little enterprise.

'The abode which Hadaly inhabits in underground. Of course, you can understand that I could not leave the ideal in reach of every one.

'I have spent years working upon her mysteries. Night after night I have sat up experimenting and, up to this day, I have kept my achievement a secret.

'Some time ago I discovered, near this very spot, two large subterranean halls, burial places of an ancient, vanished tribe. I have done over the walls of the largest vault with a coating of basalt. The mummies and the powdered bones I confined to the inner vault, which I have blocked up – let us hope for eternity.

'The larger vault I have converted into a sort of fairyland for Hadaly. She has her songbirds. You may think me a trifle superstitious, but I really did not want to leave an intellectual creature down there all alone. Everything is worked by electricity.

'Our bear coats will protect us from penumonia, for we have to go through two long, damp underground passages. We shall go like arrows. Indeed, it is most fantastic.'

The professor preceded his young friend on their journey. They walked to the shadowy spot in the wall at the end of the laboratory where Hadaly had made her appearance.

'I confess to you,' said the scientist, 'that when I visit this enchantress I take her all my anxieties. And my problems are usually solved before I come back to earth.'

While making this confession, the professor had turned a screwhead in the wall. The panels of the walls slid back.

'Come,' he said jocularly, 'in going into the realm of the ideal, we must first pass through the kingdom of the commonplace. We will now leave the earth's surface.'

The two men passed over the lighted threshold.

'Hold on to that,' said the professor, indicating an iron ring, which Lord Ewald seized. Then, taking firm hold of a twisted cord of metal concealed in the hangings, the scientist gave a pull.

The white slab of marble under their feet began to glide downward. The light above grew smaller. They soon found themselves going from humid shadows into utter darkness where there were chill odours that were foreign to Lord Ewald.

The slab continued to descend. The light above them was now only a tiny star. Soon the last light of the world above had vanished. Lord Ewald felt that he was in a profound abyss.

'What an amazing manner in which to search for an ideal,' he thought, but he said nothing, for the professor seemed to prefer silence.

Lord Ewald suddenly became all attention. For, above the rumble of the mechanism he thought he heard the sound of laughter.

Gradually their speed diminished, there was a slight jolt, and they found themselves standing before a lighted porch. An odour of amber and roses floated enchantingly on the air.

Lord Ewald saw before him a spacious subterranean hall such as might have intrigued the fancy of the caliphs under the city of Bagdad.

'You may go in,' said the professor. 'You have been introduced.'

Lord Ewald went forward, walking on the skins of wild animals which covered the floor. A clear blue light lit up the vast hall with the brilliance of a radiant summer day. Tremendous pillars, placed at intervals, supported the interior circuit of a dome of basalt, and formed a gallery to the right and left of the entrance, running back to the half circle of the hall.

This abode was gorgeously decorated in Syrian fashion. Large sheaves and garlands of silver were entwined on a bluish background. In the centre of the vault, suspended from a long golden chain, was a cluster of powerful electric lights shaded with blue globes.

The arched roof, which was of extraordinary height, was absolutely black. Against this background the light cluster appeared like a fixed star. It was a representation of heaven as it might appear – black and sombre outside of all planetary atmosphere.

The half circle which formed the end of the hall opposite the entrance was occupied by a tropic scene. Picturesque waterfalls flowed and cascades bubbled, and under the caress of an imaginary breeze wonderful flowers of the Orient grew in profusion. Birds from southern climates warbled gaily in this garden of artificial flora.

Near a pillar, her elbow leaning on a modern piano, which was lighted with electrical candelabra, stood Hadaly. She was still wearing the long black veil. With youthful grace she gave a slight inclination of her head to welcome Lord Ewald. An artificial bird of paradise was perched on her shoulder, balanc-

ing its jewelled aigrette, and apparently talking to the Andraiad in an unknown tongue.

Under a vermilion lamp stood a long table of pink marble.
At one end of this was fastened a violet silk cushion like the
one in the laboratory which held the flesh-like arm.

On a small ivory table near at hand a case filled with crystal
instruments stood open, displaying its gleaming contents. In
a distant corner there was an electrical heater, reflected to all
sides by silver mirrors.

There was no furniture except a sleeping couch covered
with black satin, and a small table placed between two lounge
chairs. A great ebony frame covered with a sheet of white
silk surmounted by a golden rose leaned against a part of the
wall.

When Lord Ewald had taken a few steps forward all the
birds turned their heads and looked at him. After a moment's silence they all burst out simultaneously into a chorus
of laughter in which was blended the shrill ring of feminine
voices. This was so lifelike that Lord Ewald felt as if he were in
the presence of human beings, and he stopped short.

The inventor, who had remained behind, in the darkness
of the tunnel, to fasten the slab, came slowly forward towards
Lord Ewald and said:

'My lord, I had forgotten. They are welcoming you with a
serenade. If I had known in time what we were going to do

this evening, I would have spared you this racket by interrupting the current of the battery which animates these birds you see here.

'In these birds I have tried to reproduce the words of old-fashioned songs and some human laughter as I thought thus to express the real spirit of progress. Real birds repeat so poorly what one tries to teach them.

'So I have found it rather amusing to catch some fine phrase or odd statement from a casual visitor in my laboratory by the aid of the phonograph and transmit it to these birds – they are really winged condensers – this is one of my secrets which I have not made known.

'Pay no attention to them. Hadaly will make them stop. I will be with you in just a moment, but I must fasten our elevator securely. I don't want it to go back to earth without us.'

Lord Ewald looked with interest at Hadaly, whose calm breathing raised the pale silver of her breast.

The piano suddenly began playing, alone, a beautiful melody. The notes lowered and raised as though they were operated by invisible fingers. The soft voice of the Andraiad began to sing to this accompaniment:

Hail! O fond youth, what can you gain?

The tears of hope shall be my dower;
Love's curses on my head doth rain.
Flee, then! Hasten! Your eyes refrain;

I'm no more than a dying flower.

Then, from the garden of flowers, there came an almost deafening noise, shouting, harsh voices of human beings, cries of admiration, foolish questions, the sound of applause, offers of money, *et cetera*. But, at a sign from Hadaly, all this stopped immediately.

The silence was broken again by the singing of a nightingale. The beautiful song, so perfect, so natural, seemed strange in this artificial place.

'A beautiful voice, is it not, Lord Ewald?' the phantom inquired softly.

'Yes,' replied the young man, both chilled and thrilled by speech from this semi-living form. 'That is the work of God.'

'Then admire it, but do not try to find out how it is produced.'

'What risks would I run if I did try?'

'God would take away the voice,' murmured the phantom.

The professor now came towards them.

'Ah,' he said, 'I see that you already seem to understand each other. Don't pay any attention to me; I don't wish to interfere; just go ahead.'

'We were talking about the nightingale,' Lord Ewald explained. 'It was a strange idea of yours to give a real nightingale to an Andraiad.'

'That is because I am a lover of nature. I liked the plumage of the bird very much, and his death, which occurred two months ago, made me very sad.'

'What! The nightingale has been dead two months?'

'Yes. I took a record of his last song. The phonograph which reproduced it is twenty-five miles away from here, in a room in my apartment in the city.

'I have attached a telephone to the wires passing over my laboratory, and a branch comes down to these vaults. It ends right over there by that cluster of flowers; in fact, it is this flower right here that is singing.'

As he spoke the professor lit his cigar at the heart of a pink camellia.

'Really,' murmured Lord Ewald sadly, 'can it be that the bird whose song I heard is dead.'

'No,' the professor replied, 'not entirely dead, since I have been able to record his song, to register his soul. I did that by electricity.'

He touched the bird, and shrugged with annoyance at the tinkle of broken crystal that followed.

Suddenly, Lord Ewald felt a light touch on his shoulder. He turned. It was Hadaly.

'Ah,' she said, in a voice so sad that it made him tremble, 'that is what I feared – God has taken away the song.'

XII.

'Hadaly,' said Professor X, 'we have just come from the earth, and the trip made us thirsty.'

The phantom drew near to Lord Ewald. 'My lord,' she said, 'will you take ale or sherry?'

'I'll take sherry, if you please,' he murmured.

Hadaly took from a stand a plate on which stood three beautiful Venetian glasses, and a bottle of wine, still wrapped in straw. Beside the wine was a box of Havana cigars.

She poured the wine into the three glasses and offered two of them to her callers. Then she raised her glass high above her head and said:

'Lord Ewald, I drink to your loves.'

The tone in which the toast was given was so exquisite that it was impossible for Lord Ewald to take offence at the sentiment.

After she had toasted Lord Ewald, Hadaly threw the contents of her glass towards the astral lamp. The old Spanish wine fell in sparkling drops on the floor.

'Thus,' said she gaily, 'I drink, in spirit, to the light.'

Lord Ewald turned to the professor.

'Tell me, Mr Wizard,' he said, 'how is it that Miss Hadaly

can reply to what I say to her? It is an impossibility for such a being to foresee my questions, or for you to have had foresight enough to have recorded beforehand the correct replies on records.'

'Please permit me to keep Hadaly's secret – at least for the time being,' Professor X pleaded.

Lord Ewald bowed to his host. Then, like a man who is surrounded by marvels, and who has decided not to be astonished at any thing he sees, he drank his sherry and placed the empty glass back on the stand.

Throwing away his cigar, which had gone out, he took another from the box on Hadaly's stand, and, following the professor's example, he lighted it at an illuminated flower.

'Do you see this swan?' asked the scientist. 'I have put the voice of Albani in that. Once, on a trip to Europe, I made a record of the great diva's singing of the "Casta Diva," the great prayer from Norma. I only regret that I did not live in the time of Malibran.

'That bird of paradise over there can render for you, through all the voices and instruments imprisoned in him, the whole of Berlioz's opera, "The Damnation of Faust." That other bird over there can recite the whole of Shakespeare's "Hamlet."

'I have only respected the voice of the nightingale, as he alone seemed to have the right; all the others are singers, musicians, and comedians to amuse Hadaly. Since she lives so far beneath the earth, she must have some distractions. What do you think of the aviary?'

'It makes the wildest imagination of the Arabian Nights pale into insignificance,' said Lord Ewald.

'Yes; the world has not begun to realize what electricity can do. We have just commenced. Soon there will be no need for cannons, or dynamite, or armies –'

'Oh, that's just a dream,' Lord Ewald objected.

'We have no more dreams!' said the master electrician, in a low voice.

He was thoughtful for a few moments, then he went on:

'Now, I am going to show you, seriously, the organisms of the new electric human creature – *The Future Eve* – which, aided by the artificiality which has been in vogue for a long time, seems to meet in full the secret wishes of our race –'

'Will you let me ask you one thing more, professor? Some thing perhaps to me more interesting than the examination you are about to make. What was the motive that caused you to create this incomparable creature?'

Lord Ewald looked straight into the eyes of the inventor, as he waited for his reply.

'That is a secret, my lord.'

'You may trust me with it,' said Lord Ewald urgingly. 'You know I had a secret and I told it at your request.'

'So be it then. Hadaly's exterior is the result of the intellectual ideal which preceded her in my mind. After you know the sum total of the reflections from which she emanated, you will be better able to understand the anatomy of this electrical being when I explain it to you later.

'Hadaly,' said the professor, turning abruptly, 'will you be good enough to leave us for awhile. I wish to say something to this young gentleman in private.'

The Andraiad, without replying, walked slowly to the end of the vaulted hall, holding her bird of paradise high in the air on her silver fingers.

'I once had a friend, a friend of my childhood; an inventor; a splendid fellow in every way,' Professor X began. 'In a few years he rose from comparative poverty to riches. He married a girl he had loved for a long time.

'Two years passed. One day he was in the city attending a business meeting. After the conference, his friends suggested a music hall.

'Anderson, that was my friend's name, was a model husband. He was seldom away from home for any length of time. However, that same morning, a foolish little domestic scene had occurred.

'Mrs Anderson, without any reason, had asked her husband not to attend the meeting. He argued with her, and, because she would not give him her reason, he went.

'At the music hall, dazzled by the lights, excited by the music, his eyes wandered vaguely to a girl with red-gold hair who was dancing in a ballet. He put up his glasses and found that she was very attractive, but he gave her no more thought.

'Later, his friends went behind the scenes and he went with them. It was all a novelty to him. There he met Evelyn Habal, the pretty red-haired girl. Anderson gazed around him absent-mindedly, without paying any attention to the dancer.

'His friends proposed for all of them a champagne supper at a restaurant, but Anderson refused to go. And then he thought of the little scene that he had had at home that morning. The affair still rankled and he decided not to return home until his wife was asleep. He went to supper fully decided to leave as soon as the meal was over.

'Piqued by Anderson's lack of attention, Miss Habal set out to captivate him. And after he had imbibed several glasses of champagne, he began to think her very delightful.

'Anderson was a strait-laced man. He adored his wife. Yet he became gradually enamoured of the charms of the dancer. The place, the wine, and the laughter were responsible.

'Mrs Anderson, conforming to traditions, sat up all night waiting for her husband. One glance at him was enough for her. It was as though an icy hand had touched her heart.

'She asked him what had happened. He explained to her that the banquet had lasted longer than he had expected, and that he had thought it better to remain with one of the party.

'Mrs Anderson turned as pale as a corpse, and said: "My dear, let this first lie be the last." She went to her room and wept.

'Poor Anderson suffered cruelly. His love for his wife was real. But from that day, his home was changed. He had a chill reconciliation with his wife, but his home soon became intolerable.

'After some weeks of misery, he returned to Miss Habal. His downfall began. He lavished his money upon her. When it was all gone, she refused to see him any more.

'Anderson changed physically and morally. He shunned his friends. Finally, he took his life. Poor Anderson!'

The professor paused for a moment as he thought with regret of his dead friend. Then he continued:

'Well, when I thought of poor Anderson and the woman who had caused his downfall, I told myself that all women are complex. They are all illusive. We are attracted to them by their beauty, wit, or other charms. They are not only illusive, but illusions.

'So I bethought: Why not build a woman who should be just the thing that we wanted her to be? Why not supply illusion for illusion?

'So Miss Habal became the subject of my observations – for I was about to try out a new and curious experiment. I went to study her.

'It is now several years since she died, but I can make her come back now as if nothing had happened. See, she will dance for you.'

The professor arose and pulled a cord.

On the large white silk sheet stretched on the ebony frame suddenly appeared the figure, lifelike, of a woman, a pretty red-haired woman.

In front of the powerful light of the great lamp was hung a long strip of gummed material covered with tiny glasses of transparent tints. These had begun to move, wound by a clock movement, and to pass through the bell-shaped lens of a powerful reflector.

It was the light from this reflector which fell upon the silk sheet. The vision with the transparent skin was a woman's photograph.

She began to dance. The movements were produced by the passing of successive photographs at a high rate of speed in front of the powerful light thrown by the reflector.

The professor touched a fluting on the ebony frame. Suddenly a flat, dull voice was heard – the dancer was singing to her fandango.

The movements, the looks, the twisting gestures, the play of the eyes and the eyelids, the very meaning of her smile, were reproduced.

'Is she not a fascinating creature?' asked the professor. 'My poor Anderson!

'See her beautiful red hair, truly that is burned gold, and her exquisite complexion, and her strange, almond-shaped eyes, her pretty fingers with the rose-coloured nails, her smile and her dazzling crimson mouth. In spite of all, nature is very beautiful.'

'Yes,' said Lord Ewald, 'you can joke at nature all you like. But I'll wager your friend found this young woman very delightful.'

'Wait!' cried the professor, bitterly.

He slipped the cord. The ribbon of photographs in front of the lamp, the living image, disappeared. A second ribbon began to unwind rapidly.

On the sheet was thrown the vision of a little, bloodless being, vaguely feminine, with stunted limbs, hollow cheeks, toothless jaws, almost without lips, the head nearly bald, the eyes sunken, and the face wrinkled.

The wretched apparition sang a coarse song in a drunken voice, and danced in grotesque imitation of the figure that had preceded it.

'What do you think of it now?' asked the professor.

'Who is the old witch?'

'The same girl. Only this is the real girl. All this was there under the semblance of the other. The other was the illusion. Art can work wonders, my dear fellow.

'Here is the real Evelyn Habal, shorn of her exterior attractions, her fine rags and tinsel.

'Can you imagine any man dying for that? How could a man be inspired with a noble passion for that?

'Now, what do you think of simple nature? We could never compete with this, could we? I ought to despair? I ought to bow my head? What do you think of it?

'Don't you think that if Anderson had seen her for the first time like this, he would still be sitting by his fireside with his wife and children? After all, that is worth everything in the world.

'What are exterior attractions? Women have fairy fingers, and once the first impression is produced the illusion is tenacious. It even feeds on the most odious faults, one clings to the chimera with one's very nails, and, often, they come to what my friend did – an untimely death.'

'Did you say that both those figures were produced by the same woman?' Lord Ewald demanded.

The scientist looked thoughtfully at his young friend.

'Ah, young man,' he said, 'you indeed have the ideal very deep in your heart. Alas, that I must disillusion you.

'Look, my lord, here in reality is what destroyed poor Anderson's body, fortune, soul and life.'

Pulling out a drawer from the wall, while the wretched figure was still performing its sinister dancing, he added:

'You will now see the spoils of the charmer, the arsenal of the sex. Will you have the kindness to light up for us, Hada-ly?'

The veiled figure of the Andraiad came forward promptly.

XIII.

'Here,' said Professor X, 'we have most of the charms of Miss Evelyn Habal. If you found them natural in the first aspect, Lord Ewald, you will have to correct your impression. She was only counterfeit.'

Hadaly raised a lighted wand above her head and stood close to the sombre drawer – like a statue beside a sepulchre – while the professor called out like an auctioneer:

'First of all, we have the wonderful hair of Herodias, gleaming like the rays of the sun in the autumn foliage; the souvenir of Eve, golden hair, eternally glorious!'

He shook out a horrible switch of discoloured hair, in which one could see that the grey hairs had been dyed.

'Here is the lily complexion, the blush of innocent modesty, the colour of the tempting lips!'

He pulled out boxes of cosmetics, creams, powders, and beauty patches.

'Here is the calm splendour of the magnificent eyes, the arc for the eyebrows, the shadow and the languor of passion, the pretty veins of the temples, the pink of the nostrils, which dilate with joy as she listens to the footsteps of her beloved.'

He threw out the curling tongs, blackened with smoke; the

blue pencil, the rouge.

'Here are the dazzling teeth, so pretty and white, which in the magic of a smile provokes the first kiss.'

He touched the spring of a set of false teeth, making them click together.

'Here is the beauty of the velvety throat, the clinging arms, the alabaster shoulders.'

He lifted up, one after another, the instruments for enamelling.

The scientist threw all the things back into the drawer pell mell, and letting the lid fall as he would on a coffin, he pushed it back into the wall.

'I think, my dear fellow, that you are more enlightened now,' he said. 'Of course, I don't mean that all women are like that, but most of those who bring men to a desperate end are, more or less. But what I want to say is, that in the end all will resemble that spectre on the screen.'

Lord Ewald was silent and saddened. He looked at Hadaly thoughtfully.

'Yes,' said the professor, 'one could kneel before a tomb, but it would be very difficult to bow before the contents of that drawer, would it not?'

He pulled the cord, the spectre disappeared, the funeral oration was ended.

'It is really not worth while,' he continued, 'to break one's home ties and to spring headlong into suicide. All for the contents of that drawer. Bah!

'With proof that my poor friend had been held by such chimeras as these, I said to myself: "This is nothing but an artificial living illusion. In Europe and America every year there are thousands of reasonable men who forsake splendid wives and allow themselves to be destroyed by an absurd illusion –"
'

'Well,' interrupted Lord Ewald, 'we will say rather that your friend's case was an exceptional form of madness that should have been treated by a physician. There are not enough charming destroyers for us to establish a general law from this adventure.'

'I have commenced by establishing it very well,' said the professor. 'You forget that you, yourself, found the first aspect of Evelyn Habal quite natural. In reality it was all artificial.

'All women who bring about such catastrophes are artificial. Very well, chimera for chimera. Let us spare the woman the trouble of being artificial.

'Let us try to obtain from science an equation of love. It will save thousands and thousands of lives.

'And by the aid of a clairvoyant named Sowana, of whom I will speak later, I discovered the formula that I dreamed of. Then, suddenly, from out of the shadows, I created – Hadaly.

'Since her creation in these subterranean vaults, I have

been waiting for a man whose intelligence I could depend upon, and who was in such a hopeless, despairing state as to be willing to brave the first experiment.

'It will be to you that I shall owe the realization of my masterpiece. You have loved the most beautiful woman, and she has brought you to such a mood that you are willing to die.'

Having finished his argument, he turned to Lord Ewald and indicated the fascinating, veiled creature.

'Now,' asked the professor, 'do you still wish to know how the phenomenon of this future vision was accomplished? Do you feel sure that your voluntary illusion will be strong enough to withstand this explanation?'

'Yes,' declared Lord Ewald, glancing at the phantom, who now appeared to be suffering from a sudden fear. 'What is wrong with her?' he asked.

'Nothing. It is a natural action. It is a child's attitude. She is hiding her face from the world.'

There was a tense moment. Then the inventor cried:

'Come, Hadaly!'

The veiled figure walked slowly, like a shadow, towards the marble table. 'My lord,' said the soft voice, 'be indulgent for my humble unreality, and, before disdaining the dream of it, remember the human companion who forced you to resort to a phantom to draw you away from a destroying love.'

As these words were uttered there was a flash, and a flood

of electricity animated the metal armour of the Andraiad. The professor touched the figure with a piece of wire held between two long glass pincers. The pulsing flame died out, and it was as though the soul of this humanlike thing had disappeared.

Then, with an irregular movement, the mechanical figure settled onto its back on the table with its head resting on the violet silk cushion.

The inventor leaned over and, taking two metal leashes from the slab, slipped them over the feet of the figure, which was now laid out like a patient on a surgical table.

He touched one of the phantom's rings. The metal armour slowly opened.

Lord Ewald started and turned pale. His nausea was more spiritual than physical.

Until now, despite all evidence, he had been assailed with doubt. It had been impossible for him not to think that there was a human, living creature enclosed in the armour.

Instead, here was revealed this entirely fictitious creature, born of science and of the patience of genius.

XIV.

The professor loosened the black veil which draped the figure.

'An Andraiad,' he said, impassively, 'is divided into four parts.

'First: The vital system, the internal part, which includes equilibrium, walking, the voice, gesticulation, the senses, the future expression of the countenance, the secret regulation of movement – or better expressed – the soul.

'Second: The plastic mediator – that is to say, the metallic envelope, separated from the epidermis and the flesh, a kind of armature with flexible joints, in which the internal system is firmly fixed.

'Third: The incarnation – or, properly expressed, the artificial flesh – superimposed on the mediator and adherent to it, and which includes the features and the outlines, together with the bony skeleton, the venous network of the musculature, and the various proportions of the body.

'Fourth: The epidermis, or human skin, which includes and implies the complexion, the pores, the features, the smile, the subtle changes of expression, the accurate labial movements in speech, the hair of the head, the ocular apparatus, with the individuality of the glance, the dental system.'

The scientist had uttered these words as impassively as if he were stating a theorem in geometry. His young listener felt from the voice that Professor X was on the point of furnishing the proof.

Lord Ewald felt his blood congeal.

'My lord,' the professor continued in a voice strangely grave and melancholy, 'you are about to witness the birth of an ideal creature, in listening to the explanation of the internal organisms of Hadaly. What Juliet could undergo such an examination without causing Romeo to faint?

'But this Andraiad, even in her beginnings, causes at no moment the frightful impression called forth by the vital process of the human organism. In her everything is affluent, ingenious and impressive. Look!'

With this, he pressed with his scalpel upon the central apparatus, which was split at the cervical vertebra.

'This is the central point of life in man,' he went on. 'It is the region of the vertebra, the point where the marrow is formed. The prick of a needle here, as you know, is sufficient to extinguish life instantly.

'Let us examine, first of all, at a glance, as it were, this organism as a whole. I will explain the details to you later.

'Thanks to the power which resides in these metal discs, heat, movement and power are distributed throughout the body of Hadaly by the network of these shining wires, reproduction of our nerves, arteries and veins. Owing to these discs of hardened glass interposed between the current and the network of wires, movement begins or ceases in one of the members or in the entire body. Here you see the electromagnetic motor.

'This spark, a legacy from Prometheus, produces respiration by animating this magnet placed vertically between the breasts. I have even given thought to those deep sighs that reflect the sadness of a woman's heart.

'Hadaly, being of a gentle and taciturn character, is not ignorant of them, nor is their charm absent from her personality. Women will all tell you that the imitation of these melancholy sighs is easy. Actresses sell them by the dozen.' The professor interrupted himself with a short laugh.

'Here are the two golden phonographs, inclined at an angle towards the center of the breast, which serve Hadaly as lungs. Through them pass, one by one, the harmonious, I might say celestial speeches, somewhat as the sheets pass through a printing press.

'A single metallic sheet contains words sufficient for seven hours; these words are the product of the greatest poets, the most subtle metaphysicians and the profoundest romancers of this century. For this reason Hadaly substitutes general intelligence for an individual intelligence.

'You see here two delicate rods of steel, trembling on fluted bases; they await only the voice of your friend, Miss Cleary. They will seize it at a distance while she is reciting, as an actress, scenes incomprehensible to her. Hadaly will incarnate herself forever in these rôles.

'Below the lungs we have a cylinder for the gestures, the walk, the visual expression, and the postures of the adored being. It is a copy of the cylinders of the highly perfected street organs. The inductor of this cylinder is, so to speak, the great sympathetic control of our marvellous phantom.

'The cylinder governs the expression of about seventy general movements; that is, approximately, the number which are at the disposal of a well bred woman.

'Our movements, except in the case of neurotic and highly nervous individuals, are nearly always the same; only the varying situations of life lend shade to them and make them appear different.

'I have calculated, by analysing their components, that twenty-seven or twenty-eight movements, as a maximum, constitute a rare personality. Moreover, what is a woman who gesticulates a great deal? An insufferable creature! One should encounter here only harmonious movements, the others being useless or shocking.

'Now, the two lungs and the great sympathetic control of Hadaly are united by this unique movement, of which the electric fluid furnishes the impulse. Twenty hours of conversation, inspiring, captivating, are inscribed on these sheets, ineffaceable, thanks to galvanoplasty, and their corresponding expression is likewise fixed in the roughness of this cylinder, encrusted, in turn, in the micrometer.

'I am able to read the gestures on this cylinder as readily as a typesetter reads a page of type backwards – it is a question of habit. I shall correct, let us say, this proof sheet according to the mobility, or changeableness, of Miss Cleary. This operation is not difficult, thanks to successive photography, of which you have just seen an application –'

'But,' interrupted Lord Ewald, 'a scene such as you imagine presupposes an interlocutor.'

'Well,' replied the professor, 'will you, yourself, not be this interlocutor?'

'How will it be possible for you, professor, to foresee what I shall ask or reply to the Andraiad?'

'Everything may serve as an answer to anything, my lord; it is the great kaleidoscope of human speech. Given the colour and the tone of a subject in the human mind, it is indifferent what word may be used in discussing it in the infinity of human conversation. There are many vague, shadowy words, of strange intellectual elasticity, whose charm and depth depend entirely on that to which they respond.

'Let us suppose a detached word – say the word *already* – as the one to be uttered by the Andraiad at a given moment. You will expect this word, which will be uttered in the soft and grave voice of your charming young friend.

'Ah! Think of the number of questions and thoughts to which this one word may furnish an apt response. It is for you to create its depth and beauty by your very question.

'This is what you try to do in real life, with a living woman; only, when it is this very word that you expect, hope for, when it would be in such sweet harmony with your thought that you long to prompt its utterance, so to speak, never does she utter it. There will always be a harsh dissonance; another word, in fact, which her natural caution will suggest, and that will stab your heart.

'With the future Alicia, the real Alicia, the Alicia of your dreams, you will never be subjected to these sterile disappointments. It will be the expected word, the beauty of which will depend on your suggestion, that your dream-woman will utter.

'Her conscious utterance will no longer be the negation of yours, but will become the semblance of the soul that responds to your melancholy. You will be able to evoke in her the radiant reality of your exclusive love, without fearing, this time, lest she repudiate your dream.

'Her words will never disappoint your hopes. They will always be sublime – provided your inspiration serves to arouse them.

'Here, at least, you will have no fear of being misunder-stood, as with the living woman; you will need only to give heed to the pauses indicated between the words. It will not even be necessary for you to articulate your words yourself—hers will be the reply to your thoughts and your silences.'

XV.

'My dear professor,' said Lord Ewald, 'do you expect me to play a continual farce? I may as well tell you, at this point, that I shall be obliged to refuse the offer.'

'Nonsense, my dear fellow,' Professor X expostulated. 'Were you not always playing a farce with the original? From all you have told me, I know that it was necessary for you to keep your inner thoughts hidden out of politeness.

'Every man plays a comedy – he deceives himself. We are none of us sincere, for we don't even know ourselves.

'Now, since Miss Cleary is an actress, and is only worthy of your admiration in that rôle, why should you ask more of the Andraiad? She will also have a great fascination in her acting.'

'That is very specious,' said Lord Ewald sadly, 'but always to hear the same words, to have them forever accompanied by the same expression, no matter how wonderful and beautiful that expression, and how beautiful that acting might be, would be tiresome.'

'Do you think that we are alway improvising?' scoffed the professor. 'Why, we are always reciting. For nearly two thousand years all our prayers have been only weak dilutions of those which were bequeathed to us.

'In every day life nearly all our phrases are repeated. You won't always think that you are having a conversation with a phantom when you talk with Hadaly, I assure you.

'Each human trade has its particular phrases, and every man therein turns around and around in this circle. A man's vocabulary, which he thinks is great, is reduced to about one hundred phrases constantly repeated.'

'Very well,' said Lord Ewald, 'you seem to have a winning argument for all my questions and objections. Proceed with the dissection of your beautiful corpse.'

The professor again took up his glass pincers.

'It is getting late,' he said, 'and I have scarcely time to give you a general idea of Hadaly's possibilities. But if you get an idea that will be sufficient. The rest is only a question of workmanship.

'See here, she has silver feet, the beautiful silver of moonlight; they are only waiting for the pink nails and the delicate veins of the living Venus. But I must tell you that, if the footsteps seem light when walking, they are not really so. These feet are filled with quicksilver. The lower limbs are filled with a liquid metal which ascends and becomes restricted at the beginning of the calf, so that the feet bear all the weight. These two little boots are of fifty pounds weight. The Andraiad, after it is covered with the flesh I have manufactured, will have the walk which is so charming in a lively woman.

'I wish you to notice that the swan-like neck is united to these impressionable wires. They control the movements of the head.

'Note the delicate finish of this ivory bone work. Isn't it delightful?' the master inventor said with just pride. 'This charming skeleton is fastened to the armour by these crystal rings, in which each bone plays with the exact value of the movement required.

'All this is controlled by the central current, according to the swaying movements of the torso, which dictates to them their personal inflections, after these have been registered on the motor cylinder.'

Lord Ewald leaned forward so as to get a closer view of the mysteries. It appeared to him as though he were looking at a friend being operated on for his amusement. He could not repress a shudder.

But the professor, totally oblivious of his young friend's feeling, gave a jerk or two to the body to illustrate his point. He appeared to have forgotten that not so long ago he had been talking, with almost human friendliness, to the figure before him.

'And here,' he went on, 'are the wires which control the gait. You can see that, when she is in this position, the insulator interposes between the generating wires and the magnet.

In her upright position, the limb which receives the spheroid on its target is the one that bends.'

Lord Ewald felt hollow in the pit of his stomach. He bravely tried to smile.

'Now, we will suppose, my lord, that you have pressed the amethyst on Hadaly's finger, because you want her to walk; then, the order to move is immediately transmitted electrically; the spheroid will move to the nearest disc, as it may chance, and the limb connected with that disc will move.

'The weight of the body thrown forward gives an impetus to the heavy boot and the foot. This causes the foot to come to the ground, in a step measuring forty centimetres. Do you understand me clearly?'

The young Englishman nodded without any enthusiasm.

The professor began again.

'Once the Andraiad's foot is on the ground, she will remain immobile in this position. But if the tension of the knee is increased and it is pulled up about three centimetres, it comes in contact with the gold target. This exerts the crystal globe and it moves toward the other target and begins the movement all over again.

'This is how the phenomenon of the Andraiad's pace is procured. It moves forwards or backwards, as the case may be, as many steps as are inscribed on the cylinder, or until it is checked by a counter order from a finger ring.'

XVI.

Great beads of perspiration stood out on Lord Ewald's forehead, and some ran down his face like tears, as he looked at the calm countenance of the master inventor. He felt the whole thing to be unreal, unbelievable.

Meanwhile, the professor had touched a small urn in the Andraiad's chest. There came a peculiar odorous mist in the air.

'Now, my lord, this perfumed smoke is nothing to be alarmed at. It is nothing but a vapour thrown off by the battery.'

As he spoke the professor lifted the Andraiad's hand. An almost blinding flash ran through the thousands of sensitive wires.

'You see,' said the professor triumphantly, 'she is an angel. If theology informs us aright, angels are creatures of fire and light, and that is what Hadaly is made of.'

The professor looked at Lord Ewald with a satisfied expression.

'This Andraiad was difficult because she was the first. Since I have written out the general formula, it will only be a matter of detail and of perfection. I hardly think that, at first, they could manufacture thousands of them, for, the first thing they will have to open will be a factory of ideals. This form is perfection.'

Lord Ewald, whose nerves were keenly on edge, began to laugh. The professor's words appeared to him an unseemly joke told at an inopportune time.

He began his merriment lightly at first, but, as the scientist joined in, the strangest feeling of hilarity came over him. The place, the hour, the subject of the experiment, the very idea itself, seemed to grow horribly ridiculous.

For the first time in his life, he found himself overcome with an attack of hysterical laughter, which echoed and resounded in this sepulchral Eden. It was some minutes before he could control himself sufficiently to speak.

'What a terrible man you are!' exclaimed Lord Ewald, hoarsely. 'What a gruesome, frightful joker!'

The professor, who was smiling to himself at the uncontrolled laughter which his young friend had permitted himself, replied: 'My lord, it is you who jests. We must hurry. Our time is up.'

At a touch on its arm, the armour of the phantom began to close. At another, the marble table began to rise. Then Hadaly stood up beside her creator. Motionless, veiled, silent, she seemed to be looking at them from beneath the shadows which hid her face.

The impression of disillusion that had somewhat come over Lord Ewald, during the professor's detailed explanation, began to disappear. His half dreamy attitude came back to him.

'Are you resurrected?' asked the professor calmly of the Andraiad.

'Perhaps!' replied the dream voice of Hadaly, coming from under the black veil.

XVII.

At the sound of the phantom's voice Lord Ewald felt a prophetic sensation, as if a greater marvel was to come. And suddenly Hadaly turned to him.

'My lord,' she said, 'will you grant me a favour, in return for all the trouble that I have undergone for your instruction?'

'Why – er – certainly,' he murmured.

Hadaly, instead of voicing her plea as the young Englishman had expected, turned away from him and moved towards the bank of flowers at the end of the hall. A large velvet bag was hanging by a cord from one of the bushes. The phantom went directly towards this and removed it from its place, then she retraced her steps to where he was standing.

'My lord,' she said, 'I believe that in the land of the living it is considered good to do some worthy deed each day. This serves to pay for the blessings and pleasures which have been enjoyed.

'It is fitting that this deed should be performed before the close in order to complete the action for that period of time. So, will you let me ask, in the name of a very estimable widow – a young woman – alms for her and her two children? Just a little contribution.'

'What does this mean?' demanded Lord Ewald of the professor.

'I have not the slightest idea,' declared the scientist, who was quite as astounded as the young man. 'But, my dear fellow, it is not the first time that she has given me a surprise.'

'It is nothing unusual,' went on the phantom. 'I am asking alms for this poor young woman who has nothing in the world to live for but her two children. If it were not that it is her duty to provide for them, she would not deign to live another day.

'A terrible misfortune has crushed her so that, even in the face of this duty, she longs for death. But a sort of perpetual ecstasy lifts her soul outside of this world and renders her powerless to earn her bread. She is indifferent to her own painful privations, but she suffers untold tortures mentally when she thinks that the children are in want.

'She is in such a state that her mind only permits her to distinguish eternal things – she has even forgotten her earthly name – she calls herself by another, which she says was given to her by some strange voices in a dream.

'Will you grant my request? It is my first. You have come from the world of the living. Will you please join your offering to mine?'

After she had spoken, Hadaly went to a stand close by

and took up some pieces of gold, which she dropped into the bag.

'Of whom do you speak, Miss Hadaly?' asked Lord Ewald.

'Of Mrs Anderson, my lord, the wife of that unfortunate man who died for the love – oh, well, you know – for the love of all those things in there.'

The veiled figure pointed to the drawer in the wall which held the gruesome objects – the relics of the woman who had wrecked the life of the professor's friend.

Lord Ewald could not refrain from taking a step backward when the Andraiad leaned toward him with the black velvet purse in her outstretched hand. He felt that her conversation was weird and her imagination sinister, but the sentiment concerning the offer appealed to the humanity in him. He reached in his pocket and pulled out a handful of bank notes and dropped them into the black purse.

'Well, professor,' he inquired, 'what is the explanation of this? Your creation questions me, answers me, and talks rationally about matters which happen down here and in the world which she has never seen.

'You don't mean to tell me that a phonograph can speak before a human voice has had a chance to make a record. You can not have invented a cylinder motor which will dictate to the phantom, which can translate thought into speech before it has been uttered by a human voice?'

'I can realize,' Professor X replied with a smile, 'that all this must seem strange, but I assure you the peculiar characteristics which you have mentioned are, relatively, the easiest to produce. I give you my word that I will prove this, and I know that the simplicity of my explanation will astonish you.

'However, I think that it would be wiser to defer the revelation of the secret for a short while, as there is something else to which I wish to draw your attention.

'Do you realize, my dear fellow, that you have never asked me any questions about the nature of Hadaly's face. Have you not felt any curiosity about its present nature?'

'The truth is that, since she is veiled, I thought it would be very indiscreet to ask,' his lordship explained.

The scientist looked at his young benefactor with a grave smile, as he said:

'The beautiful face of Miss Cleary, which remains fixed in your memory, will always reappear in the phantom's features which you are hoping to see in the future.

'I am glad that you have voiced no wish to see Hadaly's face, for I want you to retain the single imprint of that other face uppermost in your mind. It is for the same reason that I have not divulged to you the other secret – of which I have spoken.'

'Let it be as you wish, my friend,' declared Lord Ewald. 'Is it your idea to give the phantom the identical appearance of Miss Cleary?'

'Yes. So far, you may have noticed, we have not spoken of the epidermis, or the outer coating. We have only spoken of the flesh.

'You know how the touch of the arm and hand in the laboratory surprised you? I am employing the same substance now.

'The flesh of a living person is composed of certain parts of graphite, nitric acid, water, and various other chemical bodies which can be easily recognized in the microscopic examination of the subcutaneous tissues. These cohere in life under a great pressure.

'Now, in the construction of the Andraiad's flesh these elements are compounded in a similar manner. They are coagulated by the use of the hydraulic press. It is just the same as the flesh of the living.

'You cannot imagine to what a point of fineness iron has been powdered for this incarnation to make it very sensitive to electric action. The flesh transmits the orders of the current to the epidermis. These orders are, of course, those which are inscribed upon the cylinder of movements.

'Now, throughout the flesh there are what might be termed regulators or resistances. By these we can produce the subtle shadings of smiles, laughter on the cheek, and the other intricate and delicate embellishments of expression which will give the Andraiad the identity of the model.

'In order to produce the softened brilliancy of true flesh, the compound, which in its original state is snow white, is shaded with colouring matter like smoked amber and pale pink. The indefinite sparkle is produced by a mica-like powder, and this is set by means of a photo-chromatic compound. There you have the illusion.

'Now, we must experiment from another angle. I will take it upon myself to persuade Miss Cleary this evening to agree.'

At the sound of this name Lord Ewald locked up, startled.

'Don't excite yourself, my lord,' said the professor. 'I assure you it will be without her knowledge of our true purpose, and I guarantee that she will be complaisant. Her vanity will be flattered.

'Everything will be conducted in the most conventional manner. A great sculptress, a woman whom I know well, will commence work to-morrow in my laboratory. I shall ask Miss Cleary to sit for her.

'At these sittings Miss Cleary will have no other companion than this artist, who is called "Sowana." She will not idealize Miss Cleary. She will counterdraw her. She will seize the exact lines of her subject's statuesque form.

'Under my watchful eye, with instruments of the greatest

precision, she will take the exact measurements of the form, the height, the breadth, the hands, the face, the feet, the features, the limbs and arms, and the exact weight of the living being.

'Hadaly will be standing there unseen. She will remain motionless, in readiness for her incarnation.

'We will apply the carnal substance, dazzling and perfect, to the armour of the Andraiad according to the thickness of her beautiful counterpart. The substance lends itself admirably to carving, with the aid of very fine tools. The features at first will appear without any tint or shadings.

'We will then have the statue awaiting the order of the Pygmalion creator. The head alone requires more work than all of the rest of the body, because we must fashion the lobes of the ears, the gentle dilation of the nostrils when breathing, the transparency of the veins in the temples, the folds of the lips, and the play of the eyelids. The lips, on account of their delicacy and flexibility, are made of finer substance than the rest of the features.

'Can you imagine the tiny magnets that are necessary to bring an entire correspondence of the imperceptible inductors when the Andraiad smiles? Look at the thousand luminous points indicated by the vast photographic proofs of that smile.

'As soon as we have attached the flesh,' continued the scientist, 'we will then proceed to reproduce exactly the features and the lines of the body. Do you know the results obtained in photo-sculpture? Thus, one can get an accurate transposition of aspect.

'Miss Cleary will be photo-sculptured on Hadaly. In a flash, as it were, we will have a microscopic duplicate – a thing so perfect that Miss Cleary, if she beheld it, would think that she were looking at herself in a mirror. When all this has been done, another great artist, to whom I have imparted my enthusiasm, will give the final touches.

'Everything will be perfection. There will be a perfect flower of a skin, as velvety and satiny as it is transparent. Er – my lord, do you know has Miss Cleary all her own teeth?'

Lord Ewald looked up in amazement at this question; but, seeing that the inventor's face was serious, he nodded.

'That is good,' said the professor. 'With an anæsthetic of my own composition we will put her to sleep. We will then take an imprint of her teeth, tongue, and cavity of the mouth, the exact doubles of which will be transposed into her twin's mouth.

'You have spoken of the light on her teeth when she smiles – the marvellous effect. Well, you will not be able to distinguish the one from the other when the adaptation is made.'

When Professor X had ceased his exposition Lord Ewald was overcome with another attack of hysterical laughter. The young man exclaimed, between bursts of laughter:

'Don't mind me, professor. Do go on, for Heaven's sake! It is marvellous. Skeletons! Incarnations! Epidermis! Perfumes! It all is too funny for words. It really – ha, ha! – it really makes me laugh and laugh and laugh. Go on, my dear fellow! Ha, ha –'

'I understand how you feel, my lord,' said the inventor. 'It is amusing, taken from that point of view, but life itself is made up of just such small nothings. Just imagine to what small nothings love itself clings.

'Nature changes, but this Andraiad will never change. She will not know life or sickness or death! She is the supreme beauty of a dream. In her magic words there will be the thoughts of several geniuses.

'Her heart will never change, because she has no heart. So, then, it will be your duty to destroy her at the hour of your death.

'A small cartridge of some high explosive will be all that is necessary to blow her to atoms to the four winds of heaven.'

XVIII.

At this moment Hadaly moved forward from the end of the great vault, threading her way through the ever-blooming plants which brightened her sumptuous abode.

Wrapped in the clinging black folds of her veil-like mantle, with her bird of paradise perched on her shoulders, she gracefully approached her earthly visitors. When she reached the stand she again filled the glasses with wine and offered them to her guests.

They thanked her with a gesture of their heads, and drank.

'It is after midnight,' observed Professor X. 'We must hurry. However, I have a question to settle.

'In regard to your future eyes, Hadaly – tell me, can you see Miss Alicia Cleary from here with your present orbs?'

The phantom appeared to shrink into herself for a moment.

Lord Ewald started as if he had received an electric shock. He sat upright awaiting, with breathless interest, the figure's reply.

'Yes,' the dream voice murmured.

'Tell me how she is dressed and where she is.'

'She is alone, in a train,' Hadaly replied. 'She is holding your telegram in her hand. She is glancing at it; she leans nearer to the light. But the train is moving very fast, and she leans back in her seat again.'

As Hadaly spoke the last words she laughed lightly. Her laugh was echoed by the bird of paradise on her shoulder.

Lord Ewald suddenly realized that the phantom could laugh as well as if not more sweetly than human beings.

'Well, then, Miss Hadaly,' the young nobleman said, 'since you have second sight, will you be good enough to tell us how Miss Cleary is dressed.'

'She is in evening dress,' the Andraiad replied. 'It is a beautiful dress – a pale blue creation. It is of such a pale colour that under the light it looks almost green. She has on a cloak. It is open. She must be very warm, for she is using a fan that has carved ebony sticks and black flowers. On the material of the fan I see a statue –'

'This is astounding!' Lord Ewald interrupted excitedly, turning to the professor. 'It passes all imagination. What she is saying is true.'

'Of course!' said the professor, casually. 'Please talk with Hadaly, while! select some samples of eyes.'

So saying, the professor went to the far corner of the room. Lord Ewald turned to the figure.

'Miss Hadaly, will you be kind enough to tell me what that

instrument on the stand over there is used for?' he inquired. 'It looks very complicated.'

'Oh, that instrument, Lord Ewald,' said Hadaly, turning around as if to look at the object from under her veil, and then turning back. 'That is also an invention of our friend, Professor X. It is a calorimetre, and is used to measure the heat in the sun's rays.'

'Oh, yes,' said Lord Ewald, with fantastic calmness, 'I have read of that in our magazines.'

'That is it,' affirmed Hadaly. 'You know, of course, that long before the earth was even nebular some stars had been shining, let us say, from a sort of eternity; but, alas, they were so far away that their radiant light, which travels at the rate of one hundred and eighty-six thousand miles a second, has only recently reached the place that the earth occupies in the heavens.

'It appears that some of these stars have even been extinguished since then, long before their inhabitants could extinguish the earth; yet the rays that came from these stars have survived them, and continue their irrevocable march through space. It is only to-day that the light from these stars, or rather from the ashes of these stars, has reached us.

'The astronomer who contemplates the heavens often admires worlds which no longer exist, but which he can see just the same because of this phantom ray in the illusion of the universe.

'Well, this instrument is so sensitive that it not only can measure the heat in a ray of light, that we might call a dead ray, because it comes from a star that no longer lives, but it can weigh the heat of this sort of star. It is very remarkable.

'Do you know that sometimes, on a very beautiful night, when the grounds are deserted, I take this instrument out on the lawn, and there, all alone, I find great pleasure in weighing the rays of the dead stars.'

Lord Ewald began to feel dizzy. He grasped the back of the seat to assure himself that he was awake. He was beginning to assimilate the idea that what he had heretofore considered the impossible – judging from what he had seen and heard on this night – was quite ordinary and very natural. He felt a dryness in the throat which prevented him from speaking.

'Here are the eyes, my lord,' cried the scientist, now hurrying towards them with an iron box in his hands.

Hadaly, appearing to realize that she would not be required to take any part in the conversation, went over to the sleeping couch and stretched out on it.

'Here are the eyes,' the inventor repeated. 'You see the difficulties which the being of an electro-magnetic creature presents in its manufacture are quite easy to solve. It is only the result that is the mystery.'

'Right, professor!' exclaimed the younger man. 'You have

spent quite some time this evening explaining the means employed in obtaining this result, and yet, to me, the result appears to be a thing entirely apart from the means which you have so kindly described.'

'Yes, my dear fellow,' agreed the scientist, 'but you must remember that I have not given you any definite or conclusive explanations of the physical enigmas of Hadaly. I have, however, told you that, presently, some phenomena of a superior order will present themselves in her. Among these there is one which I will not be able to explain. I will only be able to show you the surprising manifestations.'

'Do you mean the electric fluid?' asked Lord Ewald.

'No; it is another fluid, and Hadaly finds herself under its influence at this very moment. One can only submit to this spirit without being able to analyse it.'

'But, really, professor,' expostulated the young man, 'I don't believe in these invisible spirits.'

'Well, that may be,' the scientist observed, 'but I will swear to you that the things that Hadaly sees from behind that veil of hers are caused by such phenomena. I have not yet been able to produce sight by means of an electric current, although such a thing may be possible. No! Hadaly's vision is not my work!'

Lord Ewald felt his blood run cold; goose flesh stood out on him. But he mastered his confusion, and asked:

'May I know something about it?'

'No! It is not for me to explain. Hadaly, herself, will elucidate the mystery to you some evening, under the stars, in the beautiful silences of the night.'

'Very well,' said Lord Edwald, 'but her conversation seems unreal. What she says seems like the shadows of thoughts to which spirits listen in dreams, but which are dispersed at the awakening. Do you think that I shall understand her?

'Just now, for instance, when she was reasoning about some stars which are called in science "bags of coal," she was rather inexact, according to my schooling. Her reasoning appeared to be guided by a different logic from ours.'

'As for that, my dear fellow,' said the professor, 'rest assured that her astronomy is better than mine.'

'One would think,' said the bewildered young man, 'to hear you speak, that Hadaly had a notion of the infinite.'

'Well, I can also assure you that she has. In fact, she has little else but that. But, to assure yourself of it, you will have to learn to question her according to the oddity of her nature.

'I don't mean in a solemn sort of way. Just lightly – in an everyday manner.'

'Will you give me an example of the questions that I should put to her?' asked Lord Ewald. 'Prove to me that she can really hold in her personality – if we can call it that – in some sort of a way, a notion of the infinite.'

The professor called to the figure. She immediately arose and came towards them, but at a sign from her master she resumed her seat on the couch.

'Hadaly,' said Professor X, 'suppose that a mythological god, quite tremendous and out of proportion, should suddenly spring out of the trans-universal ether and dart across the earth's orbit in a flash of lightning – the same impulse as that which animates you, but of undreamed-of power – so that it could make solar systems spring up from the great abyss in its passage – where do you think this power would end after it had been set in motion?'

Hadaly replied at once in her grave voice, swinging her bird of paradise to and fro upon the tip of her finger.

'I think it would pass into the infinite without more importance being accorded to it than you give to the sparks that flash and fall on the grate at a peasant's fireside.'

Lord Ewald looked at the Andraiad without saying a word.

'You see,' said the professor, turning back to his guest, 'Hadaly sees and understands certain notions, the same as you and I, but she expresses herself differently. She leaves a sort of picture in one's mind after she has spoken.'

'Well,' declared Lord Ewald, 'I give up trying to puzzle the thing out.'

'Then,' said the scientist, 'let us look at these eyes.'

He opened the iron box. Its interior seemed to dart a thousand looks at the young Englishman.

'Observe these,' continued the professor; 'see how pure the sclerotic is; note what a remarkable depth there is in the pupils. They positively disturb one, don't they?

'The action of this coloured photograph adds the personal shade to them. But it is on the iris that we must transmit the exact individuality of the look. Just a question of accuracy. Have you seen many beautiful eyes, my lord?'

'Indeed I have!' asserted Lord Ewald, 'and the most beautiful were in Abyssinia. That is, excepting Miss Cleary's eyes – the eyes that you will see soon.

'When she is looking at anything in an absent-minded fashion, her eyes are of radiant beauty. But, when she is interested they change, and the expression in them makes you forget the eyes.'

'Then that will simplify my difficulty,' declared the professor, evidently pleased, for the expression of the human look is increased by a thousand exterior incidents – by the imperceptible play of the eyelid, by the immobility of the eyebrow, by the shape of the eyelash, and especially by what one happens to be talking about, and where one happens to be. The surroundings cast a reflection. All these things reënforce the natural expression.

'Now, in this experiment, we must catch both the expression of attention and the expression of vagueness – or, in other words, both the interested and the abstract look. I believe you said that Miss Cleary always looks from under her lashes.'

'She usually does.'

'Well, I will now explain to you how we will reproduce both these looks. We now have those eyes; they are merely spheroids – the inside air of which has been submitted to a very great temperature. The moving of an object passing over one of these will be revealed on this emptiness as abstract as possible – an impression is made, but not retained, for there is no life in the eye.

'But, if we take the same eye and solder an induction wire to the sides of the spheroid with their ends set slightly apart in this emptiness, and we turn on the current, the spark will be vibrating, and you can well imagine that you are witnessing the commencement of life. The physical movement is there.

'See how clear these samples are. They are truly beautiful orbs. We can surely find here a pair that will match the eyes of our Venus di Milo.

'Once the visual point is revealed in their pupils – I suppose that you know that each person's eyes differ in the place of the visual point – once I have located this in Miss Cleary I will put a spark of electricity in the centre. This will supply the iris with that marvellous flash, that dazzling radiance, that illusion of personality.

'The mobility of the eye is easily arranged; merely a matter of suspension in a socket which will be under the control of the central cylinder.

'When I have finished with these eyes they will have quite as much emptiness or vacancy in them as Miss Cleary, but the dazzling beauty of her personality will be there. You will have her at her best.'

Lord Ewald smiled nervously. The professor replaced the eyes carefully back in the iron box.

'Of course, it is very easy to imitate the hair,' he said. 'All I need is a lock of Miss Cleary's tresses, and it will be scrupulously imitated.

'As for her skin and the nails on her hands and feet –'

'Professor!' cried the young man. 'Must you go on? Good heavens, to hear the things you love discussed like this is infernal!'

'Ah, but these are not the things that one loves,' the scientist protested; 'they are only the things that one is in love with.'

He pointed to a long box of camphorwood against the wall.

'In that box over there,' he said, 'is an exact imitation of the human skin. Shall I tell you of what it is composed?'

Lord Ewald arose and stamped his feet, which had become numb from his nervous tension.

'No, professor,' he said. 'I do not care to have any more glimpses of the promised vision until the vision itself is complete. I have agreed to enter into this mysterious adventure with you. You assure me that you will soon be able to reveal its marvellous results to me. I believe you.'

The professor bowed.

'Thanks, my lord,' he said. 'I ought not to expect more.'

A bell rang. It was a call from the surface of the earth.

Hadaly arose from the couch on which she had been reclining. She moved slowly, as if she were in a daze.

'There is your beautiful living one, Lord Ewald!' she exclaimed. 'She is just arriving. The carriage is turning in at the gate.'

'Thank you! Good-by, Miss Hadaly,' he said gravely.

The professor shook hands with his creation.

'To-morrow, my dear,' he said, 'you shall have life!'

The phantom silently bowed her head.

All the fantastic birds in the green arbours seemed to waken. The fountains began to play, and the gay flowers nodded their heads.

Hadaly made a low curtsy to both her visitors, and said in a low voice:

'Good-by, Lord Ewald; or, rather, *au revoir!*'

'Now for the earth!' exclaimed the professor, pulling on his bearskin coat.

Lord Ewald also wrapped his fur garment around him.

'We shall be back in the laboratory just in time to greet her,' said the scientist. 'Steady now.'

As soon as they had stepped on the stone slab, it started up rapidly, leaving the realm of shadows for the world of human beings. A few moments later the two men entered the brilliantly lighted laboratory. They were not a moment too soon.

'Here she comes!' Professor. X exclaimed in an excited tone of voice.

XIX.

He flung open the door of the laboratory. A tall and very beautiful young lady was coming up the steps. Miss Alicia Cleary, the living incarnation of the Venus di Milo.

Her resemblance to the immortal statue was, at the first glance, incontestable. Her aspect gave the two beholders a mysterious clutch at their hearts. Here in the flesh was the woman whose photograph had gleamed in the electrical frame a few hours previously.

She remained standing on the threshold as if surprised at the strange look of the place. Alicia, the usually poised actress, was plainly amazed.

She was beautiful. Over her shoulders was thrown a wonderful sable cloak. Beneath it could be seen a pale blue clinging gown which looked almost green under the lights. Diamonds were sparkling on her throat and hanging pendent from her ears.

'Come in, Miss Cleary,' said Professor X cordially. 'My young friend, Lord Ewald has been waiting most impatiently for you, and, permit me to say, I do not wonder at it.'

'Sir,' replied the beautiful creature, with the intonation of a middle-class saleswoman – but, at the same time, her voice had an exquisitely clear ring, like a ball of gold knocking against crystal. 'Sir, you see, I have come straight here from the opera. As to you, my lord, your telegram upset me terribly – I thought – in fact, I don't know what I did think.'

She swept into the room.

'Whose place is this?' she demanded. 'Where am I?'

'This is my home,' said the professor. 'I am "Mr George Thomas".'

The radiant creature's smile appeared to cool somewhat.

'Indeed!' she remarked.

'Yes,' continued her host obsequiously. 'Mr George Thomas. Have you never heard of me? I am the general representative of the greatest theatres in Europe and America.'

Miss Cleary started, and a smile even more radiant overspread her face.

'Oh, really,' she said, in a little nervous gush. 'I am pleased to make your acquaintance.'

Then, moving nearer to Lord Ewald, she murmured:

'Why did you not tell me this was going to happen? Thank you for taking this step; I shall be celebrated – but this sort of an introduction is not regular, you know. It shouldn't be done this way. I don't want the people who live in this house to think that I'm middle class.'

Then, as Lord Ewald stood looking down at her very camly, she exclaimed:

'Are you still up in the stars, my lord?'

'Alas, yes,' replied the nobleman, bending courteously over the beautiful creature to remove her wraps.

While these two were talking in this aside, the professor had given a violent pull to the ring of steel hidden in the draperies. A heavy, magnificent stand, lit up with candelabra, and bearing an exquisitely served meal, came up through the floor.

It was like a scene in a pantomime – a supper for fairies. The lights flashed, the silver gleamed, and the rays were reflected from the beautiful Saxe porcelain upon which the game and the rare fruit were placed. A little trellised cellarette contained a half dozen old, dusty bottles. Decanters of cordials were within easy reach. There were three seats set about the table.

'Well,' Lord Ewald observed gravely. 'I will have to make a formal introduction. Alicia, this is Mr George Thomas, the noted theatrical producer. Mr Thomas, this is Miss Alicia Cleary, the young lady of whose talents I have already spoken.'

The professor bowed.

'I do hope,' he said, in an impersonal tone, 'that I shall be able to hasten your glorious début at one of our principal theatres. But come, supper is ready, and we can talk while we have some refreshment. The air down here is very keen and gives one a good appetite.'

'That is true, and I am going to eat enough for two people,' Alicia remarked, so frankly that the professor glanced at Lord Ewald in astonishment. Then, Miss Cleary, fearing that she had said something foolish before the manager she wished to impress, said:

'I know that that's not very poetical, gentlemen, but one has to come down to earth sometimes.'

The professor smiled inwardly. Lord Ewald had been right in his analysis.

'You are charming!' the host cried, with assumed good nature. 'Now, let us have supper.'

He preceded his guests to the table, and motioned them to their places. A cluster of tea roses lightly laid, as though by fairy fingers, indicated the place for the young lady.

They took their places. But before they had tasted a morsel, Miss Cleary returned to the subject on which she was interested by saying:

'What shall I have to pay you, Mr Thomas, if, through you, I can make a début in London?'

'Oh,' replied the pseudo Mr Thomas, 'I am delighted to launch a star.'

'I have already sung before crowned heads.'

'Ah, a diva!' exclaimed her host, in ecstasy. He poured wine in their glasses.

'But, sir,' said Alicia, affecting an air of gentle reproof, but, withal, greatly flattered, 'the divas, we all know, have light habits. I am not a bit like that. However, I have to resign myself to a professional career as an actress. But, then, I suppose I shall be able to make a lot of money?'

'Undoubtedly,' he agreed. 'I drink to your success.'

He raised his glass.

'Why, how sympathetic!' cried Alicia.

Lord Ewald looked appealingly at the professor whose face appeared a smiling mask.

Miss Cleary touched her host's glass with her own. The guests drank the golden wine.

All around them there was light, on the mysterious cylinders, on the large glass disks, and on the angles of the reflectors; the rays from the lamps trembled. An impression of great solemnity, even of the occult, abruptly seized the diners. All three were pale. The great wings of Science had brushed them for an instant.

Miss Cleary continued to smile. The diamonds on her fingers flashed aggressively.

The professor was gazing at her with a look at once piercing and speculative. It was the mien of the entomologist who at last encounters on a clear night, the wonderful 'night butterfly' which will repose on the morrow in the case of the museum with a silver pin through its back.

'Miss Cleary,' he asked, 'what do you think of our opera? Do you like the scenery, the singers? They are very good, are they not?'

'Oh, some of them are all right – but a trifle worn.'

'Yes, that is so,' agreed her host, laughing, 'and the costumes are those of olden times – rather foolish. But what did you think of "*Freischutz*"?'

'Who, the tenor? I didn't think much of his voice. He looked distinguished, that's all.'

'Well, all great men – Napoleon, Dante, Homer, Cromwell – had distinction, so history tells us. They owed their success to that. But I was speaking of the play itself.'

'Oh, yes, the piece,' exclaimed Miss Cleary, with a disdainful little grimace. 'Between ourselves, it was a trifle – rather – well –'

She picked up her roses between her hands and began to smell them.

'Yes, I think so, too,' agreed her host, raising his eyebrows with an understanding look, 'and that it is out of date.'

'In the first place,' continued Miss Cleary, 'I don't like them to fire a revolver on the stage. It makes you jump. And this piece began with three shots. Making a noise it is not Art.'

'I heartily agree with you,' declared the professor; 'and the accidents follow so quickly, one after the other. I thoroughly believe the opera would be improved if they would eliminate the firing.'

'Yes,' Miss Cleary went on, 'but the thing is altogether too fantastic. And the music is awful. I came out before that forest scene that every one raves over. The whole thing is too fantastic.'

'Yes,' said her host, 'the day of the fantastic is over, I suppose. We are living in an epoch when only the most positive things have a right to our attention. The fantastic no longer exists.'

Alicia Cleary continued to comment disdainfully upon the opera and the singers. And, as she spoke, the graceless words were uttered in a voice so rich, so pure, so heavenly, that to an eavesdropper she would have seemed a sublime phantom, disclaiming by the light of the stars, a passage from the Song of Songs.

Lord Ewald, who had been chagrined by his friend's facetious discourse, became oblivious to the girl's words, and only listened, dreamily, to the sound of her beautiful contralto.

The professor stopped suddenly in his conversation with his beautiful guest. He had just caught a glance which Lord Ewald, in his dreamy abstraction, had cast at one of the young woman's rings.

Evidently he was thinking of Hadaly and her controls.

'And now,' said the scientist, turning back to Miss Cleary, 'let us speak of the début. We have forgotten a very important thing – the gratuities that you will require –'

'Oh!' she cried, interrupting him. 'I am not mercenary. I am not out for the money. But I must have it, for a singer is only measured by the amount of money she earns. And, then, I want to owe all to my profession – my art.'

'A delicate sentiment. It certainly is praiseworthy. What a heart of gold you have!' exclaimed the professor.

'Well, to begin with,' said Miss Cleary, 'what do you think of twelve thousand?'

The professor frowned slightly.

'Or six,' she amended.

His face brightened a little.

'Well, let us say something between five and ten thousand pounds sterling a year,' she said, with a divine smile. 'I would be pleased, because there would be a lot of glory.'

'How modest you are!' cried the professor, his face now quite bright. 'I thought you were going to say guineas.'

A shadow, a slight look of regret, passed over the face of the exquisite woman.

'Yes,' she said, 'I ought to get guineas, but, at a début, I suppose one can't be too exacting.'

'Well, we will arrange it,' he suggested, 'and, now, let me give you a little of this Chartreuse.'

Alicia roused herself and began to look around the room.

'Where am I?' she asked. 'This is a funny sort of place.

Where in the world am I?'

'You are now in the studio of the greatest sculptress in the country. Her name is Sowana. I rent this outer building from her. She is very famous, and it would give you quite a lot of prestige to have a statue of yourself done by her.'

'When I was in Italy I saw some statues, but they were not like anything here.'

'She has an entirely new method, Miss Cleary. One has to be up-to-date in all things nowadays. Sowana is wonderful. You must have heard of her.'

'Yes, I believe I have – I – I am sure I have,' stammered Miss Cleary.

'Yes, I am sure you have,' said the professor. 'This wonderful sculptress of marble and alabaster has an absolutely new method. A recent discovery. In three weeks she can reproduce, with exact faithfulness, animals or human beings.

'Of course you know, Miss Cleary, that all society women and the great actresses are now having statues made instead of portraits. Marble is the fashion of the day. Sowana is absent this evening because she has gone to finish a full height of the charming Princess –'

'Oh, really!' exclaimed Miss Cleary, duly impressed.

'So it is *the thing*, then, with society folks.'

'Oh, yes, and in the world of Arts. Have you never seen the statues of Jenny Lind, Cleo de Merode, and Lola de Montes?'

'I ought to have seen them,' she said, trying to search her memory.

'And Princess Borghesa?'

'Oh, yes, I remember that one. I saw it in Spain, I think. Yes, when I was in Florence,' she added thoughtfully.

'Oh, yes; princesses, and even queens, are following the rage. When a woman has such great beauty as you – I have no doubt that your statue has been made and shown in some London exhibition, and yet, I am ashamed to say that I have never seen it, or even read about it.'

Miss Alicia lowered her eyes.

'No,' she said, as if ashamed, 'I have only a marble bust and some photographs.'

'Oh, but that is a crime. No wonder you are not on the top rung of the ladder of fame. Can't you realize what an advertisement it is?'

'Well, if it is the fashion, I'm sure that I would like it,' Alicia admitted.

'Yes, it must be done, and it will only take three weeks – it will be all done by then. You must stay here with Sowana, and, while you are here, we can go over your repertoire. Then I will give you the leading rôle in a new dramatic production which I shall order. Everything will go ahead very quickly, I assure you.'

'That will be fine!' Miss Cleary exclaimed enthusiastically. 'Let us begin tomorrow. How shall I pose?'

As she spoke she lifted her glass of wine to her marvellous red lips.

'Ah,' said Professor X admiringly, 'you are a woman of the world. Now, right at the start, we will crush all rivals. We must strike the public one of those audacious blows which will resound through the two hemispheres.'

'I ask nothing better,' Miss Cleary assured him. 'I must do all I can to get to the top of the ladder quickly.'

'You have the right spirit. It will be the beautiful statue of a glorious singer. It must be something that will take the great theatrical managers right off their feet. What about "The Future Eve"?'

'Eve, did you say, Mr Thomas? Is that a new rôle in a new piece?'

'Yes. The great art will justify the statue, and your exquisite beauty will disarm the most severe critics. You know the three "Graces" in the Vatican?'

'Er – yes! Then everything is settled,' Miss Cleary announced. 'Have you anything to say, Lord Ewald?'

'Nothing,' his lordship answered, with a slight shake of his head.

'The great Sowana will return to-morrow at midday,' said the professor. 'At what time shall I expect you?'

'At two o'clock, if that –'

'Two o'clock will do very well. Now, it is to be a great secret. If it were to be noised about that I am preparing to launch you in a début, I should be pestered to death on all sides by others.'

'Oh, don't worry,' said Miss Cleary. 'I won't say anything.'

Professor X began to pencil some figures on his cuffs, and Miss Alicia took the opportunity to whisper to Lord Ewald.

'Do you think he means it?' she demanded. 'Is he really serious?'

'Certainly. That is why the telegram was sent.'

At this moment Miss Cleary's glance fell on the sparkling flower which Hadaly had given Lord Ewald, and which he had absent-mindedly placed in his button-hole.

'What is that?' she asked, putting down her glass of wine and stretching out her hand.

The professor, at this moment, arose and went over to the large open window which looked out upon the park. The moonlight was beautiful, but he turned his back to the stars and looked upon his guests.

Lord Ewald, at the question and at Miss Cleary's movement toward him, made an involuntary movement to safeguard the strange flower.

'What!' she exclaimed, noticing his movement. 'Isn't that beautiful artificial flower for me?'

'No, Alicia,' he said simply. 'You are too real for this.'

Suddenly, at the end of the room, in the mysterious corner, on the steps of the magic threshold, Hadaly appeared. With a dazzling arm she slowly lifted the draperies of velvet. Then, motionless, in her armour and under the black veil, she stood.

Miss Cleary, sitting with her back to the corner, could not see the Andraiad.

Hadaly had evidently heard the last words of the conversation, for she kissed her finger tips to Lord Ewald, who got up abruptly.

Miss Cleary was startled by his unexpected movement. She half arose in her seat, and asked anxiously:

'What is it? What's the matter with you? You make me afraid!'

She turned around sharply to see what he was looking at, but the draperies had fallen into place again and the phantom had disappeared.

Profiting by this absorbed moment of Miss Cleary's, Professor X came quickly forward and, from behind her, stretched out his hand over her beautiful forehead.

Her eyelids gradually closed. Her arms, which now appeared like marble, remained still, one hand touching the table, the other holding the bunch of roses.

She was more than ever the statue of a goddess. Transfixed

in this attitude, the loveliness of her face seemed recast with a celestial aura.

Lord Ewald bent over and took her hand in his. He found it as cold as ice.

'Well,' said the professor, turning to the young nobleman, 'I believe everything will be in readiness to-morrow at two o'clock. It was very easy, wasn't it? No one will be able to prevent this lady, without putting her in danger of death, from coming here onto that platform, and doing her best to further the experiment.

'Now, my lord, we have gone far, but there still is time to stop. It is up to you. Just say the word! We will forget all the fine plans we have made. You can speak freely. Miss Cleary cannot hear us.'

During the moments of silence which followed this declaration Lord Ewald stood gazing on his beautiful companion. Then, as suddenly as before, Hadaly reappeared, drawing back the lustrous black draperies. She stood motionless, but attentive, under the shadow of her veil, with her silver arms folded on her bosom.

Lord Ewald looked from the exquisite but earthbound being who was unconscious beside him to the elusive and lilting creation standing at the end of the room.

'My dear professor,' he said steadily, 'you have my word, and I never go back on it.'

'So be it,' Professor X rejoined.

'It is sworn,' added the melodious voice of the phantom.

The draperies again fell together. A spark flashed. The heavy sliding of the stone slab was heard as it was precipitated into the bowels of the earth. The vibrations lasted for a few seconds, then gradually ceased.

The professor made several swift movements with his hands over the head of the somnolent young beauty. Then he took his place again at the window.

Lord Ewald leaned back in his chair and tranquilly smoked his cigar as if nothing had happened.

Alicia Cleary came out of her coma with no knowledge of having been hypnotized, and took up her conversation at the point here she had left off.

'I should like to know why you do not answer me, Lord Ewald?' she demanded peevishly.

Lord Ewald looked at her with a sad little smile of pity. He forbore to answer her in kind, merely saying:

'Excuse me, Alicia, I am a little tired, that is all.'

The window had remained open. The moon was declining and the light of the stars had already paled. Carriage wheels came crunching on the gravel of the drive through the park.

'Ah, here is the carriage come for you, my lord,' the professor explained. 'The lady and gentleman to whose house you are going, Miss Cleary, are quiet, simple people, and I am sure that they will do everything they can to make you comfortable, and the inn which I have recommended for you, Lord Ewald, is one of the best.'

In a few minutes Miss Cleary and Lord Ewald had put on their things and were ready to start.

'Good night, Mr Thomas,' called out Miss Cleary, as the carriage started. 'I'll be here to-morrow, never fear.'

When alone, Professor X stood for a few minutes deep in thought, then he began to walk up and down and to soliloquize, as was his habit.

'What an evening!' he murmured. 'What an experience! This mystic female child and this charming young fellow. Poor boy! Poor, foolish boy! He does not see that her resemblance to the statue of Venus is only sickly, a contagion. He does not realize that it must be caused by some malady in her blood, some mysterious thing that she was born with, the same as some persons come into the world webfooted, or others inherit birthmarks.'

'It is a remarkable likeness – a phenomenon. But it is only a sort of elephantiasis, a pathological deformity; in her case a beautiful one. Alas, that mentally she is so common!'

'No matter, it is strange that this sublime monstrosity should have come into my possession just when I needed her for my first Andraiad. What a magnificent experiment!

'Now to work! Let the phantom live!'

Advancing to the centre of the laboratory, he called out commandingly:

'Sowana!'

At this summons the feminine voice which had been spoken in the earlier hours of the evening, replied in a clear, grave manner:

'I am here, dear master. What have you to say?'

The voice came from the middle of the room, but, as before, no one was visible.

'Sowana, the result surpasses my wildest hopes. It is magic!'

'Oh, it is nothing as yet,' said the voice. 'After the incarnation it will be supernatural.'

The professor stood nodding his head, as though he were trying to convince himself of the truth of the words which the invisible one had spoken. His hands were clasped tightly before him, and his lips moved, but uttered no sound.

Then, with a sudden movement, he pulled himself together. Pressing a button, he extinguished the three flaming arcs that illumined the room. Only a small night light remained aglow, the one on the ebony table.

Its rays shone on the velvet cushion, lighting up the mysterious arm, the most brilliant spot of which was the wrist encircled by the golden snake, whose green, glittering eyes seemed to look piercingly at Professor X.

XX.

During the fifteen days which followed that memorable evening the sun shone brightly on the grounds surrounding the laboratory. Autumn was advancing, however, and the leaves of the great oak trees in the park were turning to purple.

A great mantle of peace seemed to hang about the park and grounds. It was a serenity which was only broken by the rustle of the leaves falling and the chirp of the desolate birds.

But if peace reigned in the grounds, it stopped at the gates. Outside, the whole countryside was buzzing and bustling with curiosity.

Professor X had suspended all social intercourse and functions during Lord Ewald Celian's visit. And the world beyond his grounds was agog to find out what the great scientist was about.

The scientist remained immured in his laboratory with his assistants. He never went outside the building.

Reporters, sent in haste by their newspapers, found the iron gates closed and barred. The editors became excited. Night and day their faithful writers remained outside the grounds waiting for some item of news.

The one sign of life the reporters could see was a beautiful young woman, usually dressed in light blue or some other pale colour, walking and picking flowers on the lawn at different times during the day. But the newspaper men thought this was a trick of the professor's to throw them off the scent of his real activities.

For, what could this beautiful girl, gowned in fashionable clothes, have to do with the experiments of the great scientist?

Excitement and curiosity reached their height when it was discovered that Dr Joseph Saunderson, the famous physician, had been sent for in great haste; and that, a few hours later, the fashionable dentist, Dr William Peyton, also had been hurriedly summoned.

The rumour that Professor X was dying spread so rapidly, that it seemed as though the word had been disseminated by a flash of lightning. It varied somewhat – he was dying – no, he was not dying, but he was seriously ill, raving night and day – he had brain fever – he was a doomed man!

The stockholders of a large electric company of which the scientist was one of the founders and a director, almost went into a panic, for the stock issue on the market went tumbling downward. The price dropped until the shares were no longer worth one tenth of their original value.

But when both Dr Saunderson and Dr Peyton declared

that the vital spirits of the great experimenter had never been in better condition, and that they had been called to minister to a very beautiful young lady, the stock jumped so fast that several incautious brokers were forced to suspend their activities.

One fine night, a large package was delivered to the laboratory. The reporting sleuths traced out the fact that it had been sent from the city to the depot by rail and then carried to the grounds by a truck, but they could not discover what it contained.

But the package only contained a new blue silk evening dress; slippers of the same shade; silk stockings to match; a box of gloves, exquisitely perfumed; an ebony and black lace fan; fashionable corsets; delicate negligees; very fine handkerchiefs embroidered with the initial 'H;' bottles of perfume, and a jewel case containing diamond earrings, bracelets, and finger rings. It was a complete feminine trousseau.

But before the reporters could discover this fact, they were called away to hunt up the facts in a high-life scandal which had begun to agitate the country, and the gates of Professor X's park became deserted.

A few days after the trousseau arrived, the professor sent a trusty messenger to the city. This man delivered to a prominent wigmaker a photograph of a coiffure of large size. He also gave him some samples of hair, and measurements indicating size to the millimetre and the weight to the milligram, and a package of tissue in which the hair was to be set.

As it was an order from the famous scientist, the wigmaker began work on it at once. He weighed and boiled the hair, and set it in a form. But when he came to open the package which contained the tissue, he started back in alarm.

It was a human scalp, apparently freshly peeled off, and preserved by some new method! It fell from his hands to the floor and, almost panic-stricken, he sought the waiting messenger.

'But it is a scalp!' he cried. 'It is human leather!'

'Oh,' said the messenger calmly, 'it is nothing to be alarmed about. It was specially prepared for a very fashionable society woman, who has lost her hair in a fever.

'You must hurry with it. Here is the hair dressing and perfume which she uses. Make a masterpiece. The price is immaterial. Get your best men together and weave the hair in the tissue to duplicate nature.

'Don't overdo it. Make it exactly like the photograph. I will give you just four days to finish it.'

The wigmaker protested at the brief time given for such an important work, but on the fourth day the messenger took the now beautifully adorned scalp from his place to the professor's laboratory.

Meanwhile, although the reporters had been withdrawn,

there was still much curiosity rife in the neighbourhood, and among those who were on the alert word was passed that each morning a closed carriage arrived at the wall of the garden and stopped at a door that was seldom used. A young lady usually descended from the carriage and spent the day alone with the professor and his assistants.

It was she who walked about on the lawn at different times. What could it mean? Who could she be?

Then it also was discovered that there was a distinguished-looking young Englishman staying at the inn. He knew the young lady. He had been seen calling on her at the pretty little cottage which was owned by some friends of the inventor. She was evidently visiting at the cottage, for it was from here that the carriage took her each morning and returned her each evening.

What could the secret be? Was the scientist having a romance?

Their questions and surmises were in vain. They found no reply to the riddle. But, having nothing better to do, they waited.

At evening, on the last day of the third week, a brown autumnal day, Lord Ewald Celian sprang from his horse at the door of Professor X's abode, and, being announced, he hastened down the path in the garden which led to the laboratory.

A short time before, while he had been scanning the newspapers and waiting to receive word that Alicia Cleary had returned from her sitting, he had received the following note:
DEAR LORD EWALD:

Will you grant me a few minutes? I wish to see you.

HADALY.

He had immediately given orders for his horse to be brought and had started out. It had been a stormy day, as though nature was in accord with expected events.

Not only had the weather been inclement, but there had been an eclipse of the sun. It was still twilight and the rays of the aurora borealis stretched their sinister fan over the sky. The horizon appeared to be enveloped in the dying, smouldering flames of a destructive fire.

The air was vibrating. Gusts of wind blew the leaves in a swirl along the ground. From south to north great clouds rolled onward, looking like blankets of purple bordered with gold.

The young nobleman glanced at the sky. It seemed to him that the heavens at that moment were almost a photograph of his mental state, a reflection of his thoughts.

He hurried down the path and reached the door of the laboratory. There he hesitated for a moment. But just then he caught sight of Alicia Cleary, who had evidently finished her final sitting. He entered.

Professor X was sitting in his big armchair. He was wearing his loose lounge coat, and he held some manuscripts in his hands.

At the opening of the door, Miss Cleary turned around.

'Ah!' she cried. 'Here is Lord Ewald.'

This was the first time that he had been in the laboratory since that first terrible night, and he glanced about in real dread of the surroundings.

'You are welcome, Lord Ewald,' the professor said, extending his hand.

'The message which I received just now seemed so concise and so eloquent that I came immediately,' his lordship explained.

Then turning to Miss Cleary, he said:

'How are you, Alicia? I see that you have been rehearsing.'

'Yes,' she replied, 'but it is finished now. We were just giving it a final reading, that is all.'

The professor drew his young friend to one side.

'Tell me!' exclaimed Lord Ewald, impatiently, but in a low voice. 'Have you finished? The electrical ideal – our masterpiece, or rather yours – has it come into the world?'

'Yes,' the inventor answered simply. 'You will see the result after Miss Cleary has gone. Try to get her away, my dear fellow, and then come back here. We must be alone for this.'

'Already!' murmured Lord Ewald wonderingly.

'I have kept my word,' said the professor.

'And Miss Cleary has no suspicions?'

'None whatever. A simple rough draft of clay was all that was necessary, as I told you. Hadaly was hidden behind the impenetrable mantle of my object glasses, and Sowana has proven herself to be the genius that I maintained she was.'

'And your men – do they not suspect?'

'No. They simply saw an experiment in photo-sculpture, that is all. The rest remains a secret from them. Besides, it was only this morning that I connected the interior apparatus and made the respiratory spark function. It was most astonishing.'

'I must admit that I am very impatient to see what your creation looks like,' said Lord Ewald.

'You will see her this evening. You won't recognize her. I tell you the result is more stupendous – more marvellous – than I could have dared to believe.'

'Well, gentlemen, what conspiracy are you hatching?' the actress asked. 'Why are you conversing in such low tones?'

'My dear Miss Cleary,' the professor replied, returning to her side, 'I am telling Lord Ewald how satisfied I am with you, with your talents and your magnificent voice. I was confiding to him that I had the highest hopes in regard to the future which awaits you.'

'Well, you could have said that aloud, Mr Thomas. There is nothing in that that could hurt my feelings. But,' she continued, lighting up her words with her radiant smile, and shaking her finger threateningly, 'I also, have something to say to Lord Ewald. I am very glad that he has come.

'I have been thinking over some of the things which have taken place during the last few weeks, and there is something which weighs heavily on my mind. Just by a word, I have learned that a most ridiculous scheme has been afoot.'

She spoke with an air intended to be dignified, but, somehow, it did not seem in keeping with her true character. Then she turned away from the professor, and addressed Lord Ewald:

'Please take me for a stroll in the garden. It is important. I want you to remove a doubt from my mind on a certain subject.'

'Very well,' he agreed, after exchanging a quick glance with the professor which indicated that neither man was overpleased with the situation. 'I hope it will not take very long, as there are some matters which I must return to take up with our friend here. You know that his time is very valuable, and he had made an appointment with me for this time.'

'Oh, what I want to say won't take very long,' said Alicia Cleary, 'and I think that it will be best for all concerned if I do not say it before Mr Thomas!'

XXI.

Miss Cleary and Lord Ewald strolled out into the grounds, down the darkened avenue, and into the park.

As soon as the two visitors had left the room, Professor X's face took on an expression of deep anxiety. He evidently feared that the actress, in her foolish manner, might betray some confidence.

He hurriedly pulled aside the heavy curtains and, pressing to the window, followed them with his eyes. When he could no longer see them with his naked gaze he snatched up a sort of fieldglass, a microphone of a new system, and an induction coil attached to a manipulator.

The professor connected these to some wires which ran out through the walls and became lost in the network of others that crossed and intercrossed between the trees. He probably expected a quarrel between the two strollers, and wanted to keep himself informed before giving Hadaly into Lord Ewald's hands for safe keeping.

The young nobleman, in the meantime, was impatient for Alicia to begin her discourse. He thought of the enchanted subterranean abode where Hadaly awaited him – where, in a brief time, he would be face to face with the new Eve.

'What is it that you wish to say to me, Alicia?' he asked. 'I think that we are far enough out of sight and hearing. You know, I must return presently.'

Miss Cleary was walking along with her arm resting confidingly in that of her companion.

'Oh, I'll tell you very soon,' she replied. 'Just as soon as we get to the end of this path. It is dark there, and no one will see or hear us.

'I am very anxious about something. I can assure you that this is the first time that this thought has occurred to me. I will tell you all about it soon.'

'As you wish,' said Lord Ewald, in a resigned manner.

The evening sky was still disturbed. Long lines of red fire shot up from the boreal arcs toward the horizon. Some tiny stars, which seemed to have been in a hurry to make their appearance, had pierced their way through the dark clouds, and sprinkled themselves in the spots of clear blue ether.

The leaves rustled ominously in the park, like weird voices. In contrast, the odour of the grass and the flowers was keen, damp and delicious.

'What a magical evening,' murmured Miss Cleary.

Lord Ewald was so immersed in his own thoughts that he scarcely heard her.

'Yes it is,' he said, and in the tone there was a faint mocking ring. 'But, Alicia, tell me – what is it that you wish to say?'

'What a hurry you are in this evening, my lord. Come, sit on this bench. We can talk there – and I really am a little tired.'

She leaned on his arm.

'Are you ill, Alicia?'

She did not reply.

Lord Ewald thought it very strange that she should be so quiet. He wondered what was wrong. Did she have a woman's instinct of impending danger?

It was not at all like her. This hesitancy to speak was a new phase of her character.

She bit the stalk of a scented flower which she had picked as they had strolled along the path. All her being was resplendent with beauty. Her long, clinging gown swept the daisies which grew in the grass – belated memories of summer.

Her beautiful face was close to Lord Ewald's shoulder. Her lovely hair was a bit blown about, but this only added to its charm, as it escaped here and there from under the black short scarf she had thrown over her head. But her whole demeanour was pensive.

When they reached the bench she was the first to sit down. Lord Ewald stood looking at her, waiting for her to begin. He was inwardly impatient, as he expected to be forced to listen to a string of platitudes and commonplace arguments.

Nevertheless, an odd thought came to him. Suppose the

all-powerful professor had found the secret – suppose he had found a means to dissolve the thick mist which had obscured the mind of this beautiful creature. She was silent. That was already a great step.

He sat down beside her.

'My dear boy,' she said at last, 'I have just come to realize in the last few days how unhappy you are. Have you anything to say to me? I am a much better friend to you than you think.'

Lord Ewald, at the moment when she began speaking, was a long distance from Miss Cleary. He was thinking of an enchanted floral hall where Hadaly was, no doubt, awaiting him. And, when he heard her first speech, when he listened to her first words, he began to feel annoyed, because he thought that the professor must have, inadvertently, said too much to her.

Something within him, however, denied this. He felt confident of the scientist's judgment. And, as he thought of the manner in which Professor X had managed Miss Cleary on the first evening they met, and pondered on the fact that three weeks of more or less close association with her must have given him a better knowledge of her true self, he put the idea away from him.

What, then, could be the meaning of this new, this unlooked for, development?

Another simpler and more reasonable thought came to

him. The poet in him awakened.

He came to the conclusion that the wonderful evening must have had this effect on Alicia Cleary. In such an atmosphere it would not be difficult for two human beings, in the fullness of youth, to be filled with a greater sensitiveness, greater refinement of sentiment.

The heart of a woman is so mysteriously responsive that sometimes even the most shallow must submit to influences that are sweet and serene. Probably some great light had cast a ray into Alicia's soul.

Lord Ewald decided to make one more supreme effort to awaken the spark in this beauteous, but heretofore soul-dead creature whom he loved so deeply, so sadly. He drew her gently to him.

'Dearest Alicia,' he said, 'I have something to tell you. And what I have to say comes from joy and out of the depths of silence, but a joy drawn from silence even more wonderful than this which now surrounds us.

'You know I love you, dear. I do not live except in your presence. Oh, do you not feel all this which is immortal about us? Can you not divine the sensations throbbing through it all?

'My love for you is so great, so strong, one full moment of it would be worth more than a century of other emotions. What would I not give to be worthy of this great happiness!'

Alicia was silent.

Lord Ewald felt rebuffed.

'But, there,' he added, smiling sadly, 'this is just like so much Greek to you, isn't it Alicia? Why then do you question me? What words can I say? After all, what are words – what would all words mean in comparison to one real kiss from you.'

This was the first time in a long while that there had been any talk of caresses between them. And, Alicia Cleary, undoubtedly impressed by the splendour of the on-coming night and the ardour of the youth, appeared to abandon herself more gracefully, more fervently, to his embrace.

He felt a sudden, fierce throb of the heart. Her yielding gave him a breathtaking thrill, half joy, half fear. Could she have understood the tender meaning of his passionate words? A tear welled to his eye and, rolling down his cheek, fell onto her hand.

'Are you suffering?' she asked, almost in a whisper. 'And through me? I am very sorry.'

At this emotion, at these unexpected words, he was transported into exquisite amazement. An intense delight swept over him.

All thought of the other Alicia – the terrible one of commonplaces – went from him. These few words of kindness had been sufficient to shake his very soul – to awaken it to vast

189

heights of hope, the apex of which he knew not.

'Oh, my love – my love,' he murmured, almost desperately.

Then his lips touched hers and he was comforted. He forgot the long hours, the days of disillusion through which he had passed. His love was resurrected.

He was reborn. Hadaly and her vain mirages were now gone from his mind.

They remained silently clasped in each other's arms for some moments. Alicia's breast arose and fell in a sweet panic, as if she, too, half feared. He pressed her closely, protectingly, against his heart.

Above the heads of the two lovers the sky had become clear. The blue heavens were filled with stars visible between the scant foliage of the trees. The shadows had grown deeper and more comforting.

The dazed soul of young Ewald was again attuned to the beauties of the world. But at this moment there came to him a horrible thought, piercing his happiness like a knife thrust. He remembered that Professor X was awaiting in his vaults to show him the black magic of his Andraiad.

'Ah!' he murmured remorsefully, thinking aloud. 'Was I mad? An Andraiad! How could I have dreamed of such a sacrilege – a plaything, whose appearance alone would have made me laugh – an absurd, insensible doll.

'As if any mechanical thing made of hydraulic pressures and cunning cylinders could ever bear the semblance to one so beautiful as you, my Alicia. I will go and thank the professor presently without betraying any inquisitiveness as to his make-believe beauty. Disillusion must, indeed, have cast a shadow over my thoughts for me to have considered such a terrible project.

'Oh, my beloved! I recognize you now. You exist. You are no longer an icicle, but flesh and blood like myself. I can feel your heart beating against mine.

'You have wept. Your lips have trembled under the pressure of mine. You are a woman whom love can make ideal. Alicia – I love – I adore you – I –'

He did not finish his vocal adoration.

His eyes shining with the tears of his new-born happiness, he found Alicia's lips once more. The ecstasy of the kiss brought in its train a half breathed, subtle odour, which for the moment he thought an illusion. Somehow it daunted him; a chill of doubt flashed over him from head to foot.

It was a vague perfume of amber and roses. Yet he did not understand why it shook his inner being in this terrible manner.

His companion arose to her feet and gently put her hands on his shoulder. *Her pale fingers were laden with sparkling rings.*

Then she spoke.

Her voice was a caress – a golden toned benediction – but it was not Alicia Cleary's. It was the unforgettable dream voice which he had heard that first night at Professor X's home.

'My lord, do you not recognize me?' she asked, sadly. 'I am Hadaly!'

XXII.

At Hadaly's words, Lord Ewald felt as though all the powers of darkness had gathered their united strength to strike him one overpowering blow. He was scorched, as if he had been hurled into a fire.

If Professor X had appeared at this moment the young nobleman would have murdered him in cold blood. Everything before his eyes was in a sombre red mist.

A molten fluid rushed madly through his veins. His life of twenty-seven years appeared to him only a moment of time.

But in the complexity, the unreal horror, of the moment he could not keep his gaze off the Andraiad. His heart, gripped vicelike in a terrible rancour, seemed a dead thing in his breast.

Mechanically he contemplated Hadaly from head to foot. He took her hand. It was the hand of Alicia.

He looked at her neck, her shapely shoulders – this was, indeed, Alicia.

He stared into her eyes. They were the eyes of Alicia – but the expression was ethereal.

The dress, the shoes, even the handkerchief with which she was silently drying two tears from her ravishingly beautiful cheeks, were the usual accessories of Alicia.

It all was, in truth, Alicia! But it was Alicia transfigured. She had become worthy of her great beauty – she had realized the beatitudes of her true identity.

He closed his eyes and wiped away great beads of perspiration from his temples with the open palms of his hands. His sensation was that of the mountain climber who hears his guide shout, hoarsely: 'Take care! Don't look to the left!' and who turns perversely in the forbidden direction to find himself standing on the brink of an abyss.

He tried to pull himself together, cursing inwardly. His cheeks were blanched and he was mute with misery.

His first palpitation of tenderness, his newborn hope, and his ineffable love, had been extorted from him under false pretences. He owed that one moment of ecstasy to this terrifying resemblance – this mechanical representation of the thing he loved. He was a dupe, humiliated, utterly crushed.

His glance swept the landscape, the sky and the earth, and he broke into a nervous, mocking laugh. It was as though he were hurling back to the great unknown the undeserved insult which it had offered to his soul.

Gradually this laughter gave him relief.

Then there sprang from the depths of his intelligence a thought which was even more astonishing than the phenomenon itself. The living woman whom this electrical doll represented had not the power to thrill him. It was through this electro-dynamic being, this photomicroscopic copy of his ideal that he had realized supreme joy.

The touching voice of Hadaly had used the words of the real actress without understanding their true meaning. The phantom was only playing a part, but the soul of Alicia had passed into the rôle. The false Alicia was more perfect, more natural, than the the living personage.

He was drawn from his groping thoughts by hearing in wine-like tones:

'My lord, are you sure that I am only playing a part? Are you quite sure that I, myself, am not really here?'

'No!' cried Lord Ewald, agitatedly. 'I am not. Who are you?'

The phantom moved nearer, and gazed at him tenderly. Then, speaking with the voice of the living Alicia, she asked:

'Do you remember, Ewald, back there in England after a day of hunting, when you had been very tired, and wished to sleep, a confusing vision would come and disturb you? Sometimes you would see a face looking at you fixedly.

'You tried to explain to yourself what you saw, but you were unable to do so, and anxiety prolonged into your waking hours the dream that had been broken. To drive away the troublesome thoughts, you would arise and light up your room, and then would come the assurance that what you had dreamed had been caused by shadows cast by the old furniture, or by the flapping of the hangings at the windows. Then you would go back to bed with a smile, and drop off into peaceful sleep. Do you remember?'

'Yes,' replied Lord Ewald thoughtfully.

'I thought you would remember. Yet, I think that if you had pondered on the recurrence of these semivisions, you would have come to the conclusion that they must have been something more than dreams. At times we reach a state whereby we may receive impressions, or project our own ideas from or into another world – I mean into the infinite.

'Well, then, when one is in this fluid state of the spirit, it is given to us to realize and behold what we only imagine when we are not in that condition.

'Often it is permitted us to behold during these periods the forecastings of events which will happen to us in real life. These things, then, are not dreams, as I have said, but actually visions of the future which are projected upon the screen of our transported souls.'

At this point Hadaly reached over and took Lord Ewald's hands in hers.

'You know, dear friend, these dreams are but the supreme effort of our souls to reach out from their incarnate bodies into the illimitable realms beyond, and grasp the truths of nature.

'But when you have put these dreams away, when you dispel the vision and drop off to sleep, you have brought the spirit back to earth and lost your opportunity of solving these secrets.'

Lord Ewald pondered deeply over this discourse of the Andraiad. He could not see how its metaphysical trend could answer his question, but he listened patiently, waiting for her to reveal her actual identity.

But the radiant Hadaly continued, and it was as though she suddenly lifted a veil from the face of unseen things:

'That probably is why we know so little of the other world, because when it is given to you in your living bodies to reach this state, when you might be able to communicate with it, you voluntarily put it aside and choose to forget. So you have gone on from forgetfulness to forgetfulness.

'You have been more than fortunate. For, although you refused to investigate these foreshadowings and allowed yourself to reach a region of black despondency and despair, from where you were willing to take that last fatal step – suicide – your dream forecasts have become a reality.

'You ask who I am. Behold in me the realization of your dreams – the phantom foreshadowed in your dreams, which you so lightly put aside. I have come to you.

'I am the messenger sent from those regions which man can only enter in that state of half dream, half vision. I am from out there where there is no time or space, where all illusions vanish.

'I am a creature of dreams that you have called to being in your own imagination, and who may be lightly dismissed by some of those common sense thoughts which will leave you nothing but an aching void in my place.

'Oh, do not banish me from your thoughts! Send me not away because of that traitor, reason. Let me live in your thoughts!

'You have lived in a dream with the living. Attribute to me, then, some of the qualities of that being. Reinforce me from within yourself and I shall become alive.

'I shall be the woman of your dreams – all that you would have me be. Your dream of the living has offered you nothing but the grave; permit me, then, to offer you the happiness of heaven.'

Hadaly, swept on by the fervour of her words and the passion of her plea, pressed Lord Ewald's hands to her bosom.

The young nobleman was almost in a stupor of admiration for this wondrous phantom.

'Are you afraid of interrupting me?' she asked. 'Do not forget that it is only at your pleasure that I may live or be animated, and that your fears about me may be fatal – for your fears may destroy the ideal.

'You must choose between me, the dream, and reason. If

I have spoken to you of strange things, if I seem too grave or too serious, it is because my eyes have seen things beyond the eyes of mortals.

'See, I am talking to you like a woman, and I must become a woman – I must not remain a dream creature only.

'Oh, take me away with you; take me to England to your old castle! I long to start. I long to enshroud myself and enter my casket to prepare for the journey.

'Let us hasten! Once there, in the shadow of your great walls, you may awaken me with a kiss, if you will.'

At the end of her entreaty, Hadaly bent over and imprinted a caress on the young man's forehead.

Lord Ewald was not only brave, but fearless. The motto of his ancestral house was: 'Let others fear; not I!' and this had been instilled into the blood of his race for generations, yet at Hadaly's last words he hesitated, shudderingly. Then he resolutely set out to reason with himself.

'Ah,' he mused, 'what miracles are made to frighten the souls of men as well as to console them! What could have made Professor X imagine that this figure, which utters these thoughts inscribed on a metal cylinder, could sway me or help to dispel my gloom?

'Since when has the Divine Power permitted machines to speak? What foolish, laughable pride has conceived this phantasm in the form of a woman controlled by electricity, and hope that it would be able to introduce itself into the existence of real mortals?

'Ah, but I forget! It is only a thing of the theatre, and I should applaud it. Bravo, professor, you are indeed a genius!'

Smiling at his own thoughts, Lord Ewald leisurely lighted a cigarette.

'After all,' he thought, 'Hadaly is an infinitely superior copy of an actress. For me to pass up the sport would be an act of folly.'

However, in spite of these thoughts, he realized that he had entered into an experiment quite frightful.

While he was wrapped up in his thoughts, the Andraiad had bowed her head, and, hiding her face in her hands, was weeping silently. Then she raised her head, showing the sublime countenance of Alicia, and said, her voice trembling with tears:

'So, my lord, you refuse me! You have called me out of the dream world only to banish me to it again. Just one little thought from you could have invested me with life, but, all powerful though you be, you have disdained to use the power. You prefer a conscience which causes you grief. You scorn the divine, and the ideal in captivity intimidates you!'

And, turning away from him, Hadaly, bowed in grief, moved away. The rising moon was shining gently through the tree tops, and raising both her arms toward it, she cried:

'Oh, moon, you that brings so much of hope, I had so longed to live that I might know of love beneath your tender light. But all is lost, I must relinquish life, and return to death.'

Then, wiping her tears away, she suddenly faced Lord Ewald, and said:

'Good-bye, my lord. Go, leave me, and rejoin the realities of the world. You may think of me as merely a curiosity upon which you have looked. You are quite sensible in your choice.

'Go! Forget me if you can. But I warn you that it will be impossible. He who has looked upon an Andraiad as you have upon me can never forget her. You have killed your ideal and the memory will ever remain with you as a constant punishment for the indignity offered to the divine.

'I will return to my beautiful cavern. Farewell to you who will know no more of joy in life!'

She walked towards the path and on in the direction where Professor X was keeping vigil. Sobbing, she pressed her handkerchief to her lips.

Her blue form slowly passed among the trees. The light of the moon, falling upon it, gave her the aspect of a spirit. Then she turned and, with a graceful movement, silently raised her hands to her lips and tossed Lord Ewald a double kiss. It was her final gesture of despair.

And now, literally in spite of himself, Lord Ewald rushed down the path and rejoined her. Drawn by an irrestible force, he threw his arm about Hadaly.

'Spirit, phantom, Hadaly, it is settled!' he exclaimed. 'It is true that I do not deserve to have your sweet presence in place of that other earthly one, but I accept it. I wish you to live, for I realize that in comparison the living one is the phantom, and that you are real.'

Hadaly put both her rounded arms around Lord Ewald's neck and permitted him to press her closely to him.

An infinite grace, languid and ravishing, emanated from her like a magnetic radiance. She rested her head on his shoulder and looked at him from under her lids with a beatific smile.

She seemed to be welding her soul with his in their enchained eyes. Finally, she placed on his lips a kiss that was entirely virginal.

'At last!' Hadaly said in a voice that was more spiritual flame than sound. 'At last I am born!'

XXIII.

A few moments later Lord Ewald entered the laboratory with Hadaly on his arm.

Professor X was standing, his arms crossed before him, in front of a long ebony coffin. The two sides of the box were open, showing black satin upholstering. The interior was moulded in the form of a woman.

One might have thought it an Egyptian casket perfected by modern methods, for it was worthy of Cleopatra herself. On the right and left sides a dozen strips of metal were fastened and in the interior of the box could be seen a papyrus roll, a manuscript and the crystal wand.

Withdrawing her arm from her protector's, Hadaly stepped to one side and stood motionless, while Lord Ewald advanced to the professor and said:

'My friend, this Andraiad is a present that only a semigod could offer. Never in the bazaars of Bagdad could such a slave have been found for the Caliphs.

'No other enchanter could have created such a vision. Never did Scheherazade imagine such a vision in her tales of the Thousand and One Nights.

'No money could persuade me to part from this masterpiece. If, at first, I was dismayed, admiration has triumphed over that.'

'You accept her then?' the professor inquired, smilingly.

'I would be mad to refuse her,' the young man replied, offering his handclasp as a pledge of agreement.

'Will you have supper with me, both of you?' asked the scientist. 'If you will, we will take up the conversation where we left off on that first night. You will see, my lord, that Hadaly's replies will be entirely different from those of her model.'

'No, thanks,' Lord Ewald objected. 'I am in a great hurry to become the guardian of this divine enigma.'

'Farewell then, Hadaly,' the professor said. 'When you are over the seas, you must sometimes think of your subterranean vault where we have often talked of the one who would come to awaken you to the pale existence of a human being.'

'Ah, my dear master,' replied the Andraiad, bowing humbly before the great electrician, 'my resemblance to the mortals and my place among them will never go so far as to make me forget my creator.'

'That is fine, Hadaly, I thank you.'

Professor X then turned to Lord Ewald and asked: 'And what about the living one?'

'On my word, I had forgotten her!' the young nobleman exclaimed ruefully.

'She went away in a very bad frame of mind this evening,'

the professor said. 'You had scarcely gone for the walk with Hadaly when she returned here, absolutely herself, and free from all influence.

'Well, you should have heard her flow of words! It made it impossible for me to hear what you two were saying out there in the park; and I had just placed instruments in position so that I might listen.

'However, I see that Hadaly, even in her first moments of life, has shown herself to be worthy of our expectations. Goodness knows what we may expect of her in the years to come.

'Miss Cleary informed me in very strong terms that she renounces the new rôles which I had prepared for her, because the prose was too difficult for her to memorize. She declared that the words ossified her brain. Her modest wish now is to enter vaudeville, for which she has a sufficient repertoire. She believes that she will have a rapid success.

'As for the statue, she told me to speak to you about forwarding it to London, as you were making preparations for your departure tomorrow. She instructed me to ask a stiff sum for it, as she knew that you would not bargain with an artist. Then she bade me good-by, and told me that if you should come here by chance that she would see you later about the arrangements.

'Now, my dear fellow, once you are in London you will

have nothing further to do than to see that she is started in her chosen profession. Then a letter, accompanied by a substantial gift, will be all that is necessary.'

Hadaly, who had been listening attentively, now said to the scientist:

'You will come to see us at Athelwold, dear master, will you not?'

Lord Ewald could not repress a start when he heard her express these natural words. Then he noticed a strange thing. Professor X had been more amazed at Hadaly's words than he, himself, had been.

'What is the matter, professor?' asked Lord Ewald.

Professor X put his hands to his forehead for an instant, then, drawing aside the hem of the Andraiad's gown, he pressed his fingers heavily on the heels of her slippers.

'I am unchaining Hadaly,' the inventor explained. 'From now on she belongs to you. In the future it will be only the rings and the collar on the neck that will animate her.

'While we are on this point, you will find the manuscript in the casket. After reading it you will understand into what mysteries you will be able to delve during the sixty hours inscribed on the cylinder. Hadaly will be a continual surprise.'

'My dear professor,' said Lord Ewald, 'as far as I am concerned you may destroy the manuscript. I believe that Hadaly is a real phantom, and I no longer wish to know what it is that animates her. I hope that I shall even forget what you have already told me about her.'

At these words, Hadaly tenderly pressed the young man's hands and, leaning nearer to him, while the scientist was still kneeling at her feet, whispered:

'Don't tell him what I told you out there just now. That was for your ears only!'

The professor arose with two small brass buttons which he had unscrewed from the heels of Hadaly's slippers. She trembled throughout her whole being until he touched a pearl in her collar.

'Help me,' she said simply, leaning her head on Lord Ewald's shoulder.

The young man supported her gravely, and when she regained her composure she walked to the casket and smilingly drew aside the cover. Then, without hesitation, she reclined in the sable mould.

After having wound the thick linen bandage round her forehead, she tightly hooked the lengths of silk about her body, arranging herself in such a manner that no shock could disturb her.

'My friend,' she said, addressing Lord Ewald, 'after the crossing, you will awaken me. Until then as of old, we will see each other in the world of dreams.'

She closed her eyes, as if in sleep.

Professor X closed the coffin tightly. A silver plate inscribed with Lord Ewald's coat of arms was fastened on the top, bearing the name *Hadaly* engraved in Oriental characters.

'Now,' said the professor, 'the sarcophagus will be placed presently, as I have told you, in a large square crate with sides well padded. We are taking this precaution to avoid any suspicions. Here is the key of the casket, and the invisible lock which permits the spring to unbend is this tiny black star directly above the head of the Andraiad.

'Now,' he added, pulling a chair forward for his guest and one for himself, 'let us have a drink.'

The scientist pressed a crystal knob, and instantly several flaming arcs flashed their light over the room, creating the effect of a sunlit day. Handing a glass to Lord Ewald he exclaimed:

'I drink to the impossible!'

Lord Ewald touched glasses as a sign of acquiescence.

'There is one question which I must ask,' the young nobleman said. 'You told me that a woman, an artist, helped you in your work. I believe you said that her name was Sowana. It was she who helped to measure and weigh and to calculate, limb for limb, the living model.

'Miss Cleary told me that she was a very pale creature, of uncertain age, who spoke little, was always dressed in black, and once must have been very beautiful. She said that this strange woman kept her eyes always half closed, but saw clear-ly, and that she moved as if mesmerized. Alicia also told me that sometimes this woman worked with a live electric torch as if she intended to design her statue with the flashing light.'

'What do you want to know about her?'

'I wanted to know who she is. From what I have heard she must be a marvellous woman.'

'Sowana is Mrs Anderson,' the professor replied, gravely. 'The widow of my dead friend. She was penniless, and I did all that I could to help her. After his death she became very ill. She had an incurable disease called sleeping sickness.

'I went to see her occasionally, and I was surprised to find that during her trances she was able to talk and reply to all my questions. I determined to try to cure her.'

'To cure her!' exclaimed Lord Ewald. 'You mean transform her?'

'Well,' admitted the professor, 'perhaps you are right. You may have noticed that when I used my power over Miss Cleary the other evening it was very easy. You have seen hypnotism before, so you will not doubt that there is existent a nervous current or fluid exactly corresponding to electricity.

'I do not know how the idea came to me to resort to mag-netic action. I worked upon her almost every day for about two months. I learned the surest methods, and gradually the known phenomena were produced one after the other.

'At the present day they remain still unexplainable, but in the near future they will not appear strange. Then Mrs Anderson began to have spells of clairvoyance, absolutely enigmatical, in these deep sleeps. She became my great secret. Owing to the state of intensified torpor in which the patient had fallen, I had the chance to develop this hypnotic attitude of mine to an intense degree.

'Between Mrs Anderson and myself there became established a current so subtle that I was able to penetrate metal with it. I magnetized a piece of metal with this fluid or current, and then fashioned it into two rings – this sounds like mere magic, doesn't it? – and it sufficed to estabish a communicating current between us. If Sowana had on one ring, and I had on the other, even though she were asleep twenty miles away, we could converse.

'This savours of the occult, but I cannot tell you how many times I have been able to make her hear and obey me, how many times she has spoken to me, just holding the ring, in a very low voice, when she was far away.

'In one of her trances she told me that, although her name on earth was Annie Anderson, her real self for a long time had been called Sowana.

'Not only her name, but her whole nature, was changed. Mrs Anderson had been a dignified, fairly intelligent woman; but, after all, her intelligence had been limited. However, in her sleep, with her name changed, she suddenly became a person of great talent and unknown powers. This vast knowledge, this strange eloquence, this being penetrated with a new personality of Sowana, are things that cannot be explained, for Mrs Anderson is, physically, the same woman. The duality is an astounding phenomenon, but this duality has been seen – in lesser extent – in persons under the influence of hypnotizers.

'There came a time when I decided to reveal the relics of Miss Evelyn Habal, the woman who destroyed her husband. When I showed them to her I gave her a rough idea of my conception of Hadaly. You cannot imagine with what sombre joy Mrs Anderson seized upon this novel idea. She encouraged me in my scheme. She insisted that I should get to work at once.

'So I put all my other work aside to devote my time to this experiment. When the complexities of the Andraiad's organisms were executed, I assembled them and showed them to her.

'At this sight Mrs Anderson became strangely exhilarated. She insisted that I must explain to her the most secret of the mysteries, so that she could familiarize herself with them against the day when she might be able to reanimate herself in the Andraiad and to incorporate herself in her supernatural state.

'Impressed with this vague idea, I taught her all that I knew by building for her instruction a set of apparatus similar to that of Hadaly's movements. When Sowana had completely mastered it, one day, without warning, she sent the Andraiad here to me while I was at work.

'I declare to you that its appearance gave me the most frightful shock I ever had in my life. The completed work terrified the workman!

'Then came to me the daring idea of incorporating the phantom in the double of a woman. Thenceforth I calculated all my steps with the utmost precision, so that I could offer a finished product to any one daring enough to accept.

'You must notice that there is nothing chimerical in the creature. It is indeed an unknown being. It is Hadaly, the ideal who, under the veils of electricity – in the silver armour simulating feminine beauty – has appeared to you. Although I thoroughly know Hadaly, I swear to you I do not so know Mrs Anderson – Sowana – or her powers.'

Lord Ewald was startled at the grave tone of the wizard, who continued thoughtfully:

'Down there, hidden among the shadowy leaves and the floral lights of the subterranean cavern, Sowana, with closed eyes herself, incorporated in some marvellous manner the power of sight into Hadaly. In her icy hands Sowana held the wires which controlled the Andraiad, and, although she was in the flesh like a corpse, she has through Hadaly walked and spoken in that strange, far-off voice.

'Sometimes she did not speak aloud – she merely vibrated her words on her lips; nor was it necessary for me to do more. But even more wonderful yet was her ability to understand what we were thinking about.'

While the professor was speaking, Lord Ewald kept leaning nearer and nearer towards him, drawn by his interest in the subject. But here he interrupted with a sudden gesture:

'From where does this creature hear? From where does she speak? In fact, with whom are we dealing?'

'As I have told you before,' Professor X replied, 'there are many things which so far cannot be explained, but I will refresh your memory and give you an example of what I mean.

'Do you remember how Hadaly looked at Miss Cleary's photograph when I projected it on the frame? It was perfectly natural, wasn't it? Then, do you remember her strange explanation of the apparatus in the cavern, and her accurate description of Miss Cleary on the train? Do you know how this mystifying clairvoyance was brought about?

'Well, I can explain that. Because of your great admiration for Miss Cleary, her personality has made a permanent impress upon you – magnetized you, so to speak – in the same way that I magnetized the metal for the rings which I have described.

'Do you remember that Hadaly took your hand before describing Miss Cleary? That was because it was necessary for her so to do in order to establish contact with the magnetism with which you are imbued. As soon as this was done it was perfectly easy – just the same as between Sowana and myself.'

'Is it possible?' breathed Lord Ewald.

'Yes,' replied the scientist; 'and there are many, many other "impossible" things which daily materialize around us. I can well say that I am never surprised, as I am one of those who never forget that the universe was created out of a quantity of nothingness.

'But, of course, we have here something to marvel at. Sowana, lying helpless and sightless on a cushion, has been able to project her feelings, speech, and powers of reasoning into Hadaly – to create in her a veritable other woman. This is a phenomenon of superclairvoyance.'

'One moment,' interrupted Lord Ewald. 'What you have said interests me greatly. Since I have been here I have seen you transmitting messages through the medium of space without any wires. Is it possible that electricity alone can transmit its messages to distances and heights without limit, as long as there are established contacts at those distances? How can that be done?'

'It is very simple,' declared the professor. 'In the first place, distance is, in truth, only a sort of illusion. Then, experimental science has already established many fundamental facts, such as the power of hypnotism, thought transference by personal magnetism from one human being to another, *et cetera*. These are all recognized and utilized by some of our leading physicians.

'Then, we have certain metals and chemicals which give off currents and act upon bodies – even at a great distance away – and electric magnets exert great powers of attraction, such as the lines of magnetism between the poles; and all things that pass between these lines or enter the paths of these currents are affected by them.

'Now, I believe that in the case of Sowana we have found a demonstration of a new fact. It has been possible for her, while in these spells of clairvoyant sleep, to project her magnetism upon Hadaly to such an extent that the phantom has become permanently imbued with it – or, in other words, she has become animated by it – an incarnation of Sowana herself.'

'An incarnation!' murmured Lord Ewald in surprise.

'Yes. Let us say an incarnation of idealized humanity. Now, when you have arrived at your castle, and you have given to Hadaly her first glass of water and her pastilles, you will be surprised to see what a really accomplished phantom she will be.

'As soon as her habits and presence have become familiar to

you, you will have a very interesting interlocutor, for if I have furnished physically a terrestrial and illusory body, Sowana has superimposed and injected into my creation a soul which is unknown to me.

'So you have incorporated forever a being from the other world. There is centralized in your Andraiad forever, irrevocably, a mystery that it would be impossible for us to imagine.'

XXIV.

The scientist abruptly arose and walked about, as if to quiet the sinister suggestions which had come to his mind. Lord Ewald watched him with a half dreamy expression.

Professor X suddenly pointed to the clock. It was 9 P.M.

'And now, my lord,' he said, 'I have kept my word. My work is done, and I believe that my creation is more than a common copy of a human being. Tell me truly, in comparison between the illusion and the reality, do you think the illusion is worth living for?'

Lord Ewald drew his pistol and handed it to the scientist.

'My dear wizard,' he said, 'allow me to offer you this pistol as a souvenir of our second meeting. I have no use for it, and you well deserve it as a trophy. My dear friend,' Lord Ewald continued, 'I am afraid that you have made a great sacrifice for me. I am robbing you of a superhuman masterpiece – stealing your greatest treasure.'

'Not so,' replied the inventor, forcing a smile. 'You see, I still have the formula. But,' he added sadly, 'I shall not fabricate any more Andraiads. My subterranean halls will serve to hide me when I am trying other less dangerous experiments. And now, my lord, a toast! You have chosen the land of dreams. Carry your phantom there. I am destined to be chained to the realities of life.

'Some of my trusted men will escort you and your precious luggage onto your ship, the *Britannia*. The Captain is a friend of mine, and has already been notified. Perhaps some day we may meet at your castle. Write to me. Now, farewell!'

The two men clasped hands fervently.

A few moments later Lord Ewald rode slowly down the path, where he was joined by a closed truck guarded by three men. The strange procession soon disappeared in the direction of the depot.

Left alone in his laboratory, Professor X began to pace up and down, muttering to himself. Something seemed to be troubling him, for he stopped once, rubbed the ring on his finger, and then began to stride again.

He shook his head wonderingly, and then walked quickly to the black, concealing hangings. He ulled the curtains back on their rings.

Stretched out, all robed in black, and apparently asleep on a large red sofa placed on huge disks of glass, was the form of a slender woman, no longer young. Her beautiful black hair was streaked with gray. Her fine cut features and the pure oval form of her face seemed set with an unnatural calmness. Her hand, dropping to the carpet, still held a sort of mouthpiece.

'Ah, Sowana,' the professor murmured, 'we have at last

done the impossible. This is the first time that science has been able to prove that she can cure man – of love.'

As the figure made no reply, Professor X hurriedly bent and lifted her hand. Its icy touch startled him. He leaned closer to the prostrate form.

The pulse had stopped. The heart was still.

Forcefully, desperately he made magnetic signs over her forehead; but it was in vain.

At the end of an hour of furious, tireless efforts he was forced to concede that she who seemed to be asleep had passed forever from the land of the living.

He bowed his head in grief. Inexorable fate had taken its toll, a soul for a soul.

XXV.

A week later, when Professor X was alone in the laboratory, his glance fell upon the glaring headlines in an evening newspaper, which shrieked:

GREAT DISASTER AT SEA!
S.S. BRITANNIA LOST!!
SEVENTY-TWO PERISH!!!

Aghast, the scientist perused the account of the sad happening, his prophetic glance leaping here and there among the paragraphs:

Fire broke out in the stern about two o'clock in the morning, presumably in the hold where there was a large store of mineral oils and highly inflammable essences, from some unknown cause.

It was a very rough sea. The steamer, since leaving sight of land, had run into a series of gales. Tremendous waves towered high above the liner, which at times seemed to have sunk into the depths of the ocean, and crashing down upon her decks wrought havoc.

The steamer fought her way bravely through the waves,

but the sheet of flames quickly spread over her and into her baggage hold. There was such a high wind that the captain soon saw that the vessel was doomed.

Terrible scenes took place. The women and children shrieked in despair as they retreated before the advancing flames.

The captain ordered the lifeboats to be lowered, and this was done in five minutes, but there was such a terrific rush for them that many persons were injured.

The women and children were lowered first.

But, during these scenes of horror, a strange event took place. A young Englishman, Lord Ewald Celian, tried to force his way into the baggage hold through the midst of the flames. He fought bravely against those who tried to keep him from entering, and after he had knocked down two of the crew, it took five men to hold him from rushing to his death into the fire.

While struggling with those who sought to detain him, he offered his entire fortune to any one who would help him to save a crate which enclosed some precious object. It was quite impossible to do this. The crate, which was stored in the hold where the fire was raging, could not have been taken off the steamer, as the lifeboats were more than crowded with passengers.

After a great struggle, for he showed extraordinary strength, the young man was at last bound hand and foot and put aboard the last lifeboat.

The boat he was in was rescued by the French steamship *Le Redoutable* about six o'clock in the morning.

The first lifeboats with the women and children were upset by the rough sea. So far, it is learned seventy-two were drowned.

Afterward came the list of those who had perished. The first name was that of Miss Alicia Cleary, actress.

Professor X reread every detail of the terrible disaster and the dreadful ordeal that Lord Ewald had gone through in his attempt to save Hadaly.

When he had finished reading, his eyes wandered to the ebony table. He put out the lights.

Again the moon was shining, and its rays fell upon the rounded arm and the white hand with its sparkling rings, and once more the green, ominous eyes of the snake glittered at him.

With a feeling of intense sadness he gazed through the window, and for some time listened to the wind whistling amid the branches of the trees.

Then he raised his eyes to the starry skies – to the infinite mystery of the heavens – and he shuddered – with the cold, no doubt. His was the terrible heartbreaking silence of a strong man in utter loneliness.

Lightning Source UK Ltd.
Milton Keynes UK
UKOW02f2315010816

279714UK00001B/59/P